the EPiC FAiL of arturo zamora

the EPiC FAiL

of arturo zamora

PABLO CARTAYA

Viking

VIKING
An imprint of Penguin Random House LLC
375 Hudson Street
New York, New York 10014

First published in the United States of America by Viking,
an imprint of Penguin Random House LLC, 2017

LIBRARY OF CONGRESS CATALOGING-IN-PUBLICATION DATA IS AVAILABLE
ISBN: 9781101997239

Printed in U.S.A.   Set in ITC Esprit Std   Book design by Kate Renner

10 9 8 7 6 5 4 3 2 1

To Abuela and Abuelo,
this is my love letter to you.

*"But love, like the sun that it is,
sets afire and melts everything."*

—José Martí

*THOUGHTS: ON LIBERTY, SOCIAL JUSTICE,
GOVERNMENT, ART, AND MORALITY*
(translated by Carlos Ripoll)

note to self

I'm officially resigning from love. Time in a cell will do that to a kid. For the record: I didn't do it. Well, I didn't mean for what I did to blow up in my face. This should have been the best night of my life. I was going to save the restaurant. Save the town. Get the girl. Make Abuela proud. I imagined myself riding a tan horse into the summer sunset, swatting any mosquito that tried to sting my awesomeness. Instead I'm locked in a small room that smells like chorizo and stale popcorn while my archenemy continues to brainwash the community with reggaeton and free sunscreen.

I'm sitting on a cracked vinyl sofa, staring out at my abuela's restaurant from a tiny window while I await my sentence. The only thing I've learned from this crazy course of events is that no matter how much we try to believe David beat Goliath, the reality is that the big guy always wins. Even if the big guy is actually a five-foot-three, flamboyantly dressed land developer with stupendously gelled hair. My little slingshot didn't even bruise his forehead. I also learned that love is a giant pretzel. Twisty. Salty. It leaves you dry and thirsty.

These pages contain every detail—well, most details. I'll leave stuff out like I brushed my teeth but didn't floss, or I had a sandwich, or it was crazy humid that day in the park, which is why I wore a tank top, etc. But the big details of my epic fail are all here. Everything. Todo.

So let me start the puro desastre, the, like, total meltdown, from the beginning: three Sundays ago at our weekly family dinner at Abuela's restaurant, La Cocina de la Isla.

1

when guts fry

FOR MY ENTIRE life, La Cocina de la Isla has closed on Sundays. Year after year customers have begged Abuela to open the restaurant, but she never has. She claimed Sundays for the Zamoras, and that was that. No more discussion.

Ever since she'd handed over cooking duties to my mom, her oldest daughter, Abuela took her place on one of the sofas in the lounge area, smiling and surveying the whole scene. The chaos of so many people moving about and talking over each other didn't seem to bother her at all. She looked happiest when the entire Zamora clan crammed itself into La Cocina.

My cousins Yolanda and Mari traded high school

chismes on the outdoor patio. Martín and Brian sat at the bar area next to the kitchen to watch TV, flipping from MMA to basketball to hockey to baseball without settling on anything for more than three minutes.

Benny and Brad, my younger cousins, zipped around tables, pretending to be superheroes until they were scolded by my uncle for knocking over a chair. A few of my third cousins, two of my dad's best friends from high school, and cousins who I called cousins (but weren't really my cousins) sat around in different spots, waiting for food to be served.

My dad brought out the urns containing my abuelo, tío abuelo, *and* my tataraabuelo (yes, my *great-*grandfather) and carefully lined them up on the small service bar next to the dinner table, where we would eventually sit for our meal. Yep, even the dead joined us "in spirit." The whole family was there, and everyone was in a really good mood.

I was excited for a bunch of reasons. It was the Sunday before the official start of summer, and summer meant hanging out, swinging on banyan trees, looking for manatees in the canals throughout Canal Grove, eating churros (because let's be real: those deep-fried sugary sticks are all kinds of delicious), listening to music, and jumping around in Bren's bounce house. Yeah, I know I'm thirteen, but there's just something about a bounce house that makes me feel awesome.

I had a full week to chill out with my best friends, Mop and Bren, before they both left town, and even though I'd be working at the restaurant a few days a week, it seemed like summer was off to a good start.

Mop and Bren were honorary Zamoras and almost always attended Sunday dinner. They showed up a little late today, popping in from the patio entrance. Bren walked toward me, his arms extended to give me a hug.

"¡Hermano!"

I half hugged him and stared. It must have taken him hours to put his outfit together. That was probably why they were late.

"What are you wearing, Bren?" I asked.

"I know," Mop said, shaking his head. "I tried to tell him. I think he dressed up for Vanessa."

Bren had been in love with my cousin Vanessa for as long as I could remember. She barely knew he existed.

"What?" Bren said, pulling at the collar of his shirt, which opened into an embarrassingly deep V. "Too formal?"

"Dude, you're wearing sunglasses."

"So?"

"We're inside."

"It's to keep the glare out, homie. The 305 can get pretty bright."

"Stop talking like Pitbull. You are *not* Pitbull!" Mop cried, and slapped his forehead.

Last year Bren tried to shave his head like Pitbull but ended up with just one side of his head shaved because his mom caught him before he could finish. It took six months for the hair to grow back.

"At least take off the sunglasses," I said. "Abuela doesn't like that."

Bren gave a nod, dropped his glasses to the edge of his nose, and channeled Pitbull. "Dale."

Mop and I shook our heads and waited for Bren to put the glasses into his blazer pocket before going to the lounge area to greet the rest of the family.

When we got there, I noticed someone at the front door, knocking politely. Through the windowed double doors, I made eye contact with a tall, reddish-brown-haired, honey-eyed girl waving and smiling with a mouth full of tiny colorful braces.

"Oh, they're here, everyone!" Vanessa announced as she went to unlock the door. "As the official orientation liaison to Sunday Family Dinner at La Cocina de la Isla, I'd like to welcome the Sánchez family! Carmen, you and I were, like, six when you last came to Miami, right?"

"I think so," said Carmen as she stood at the door and looked around. She said words a little funny, the way I do when I try to speak Spanish.

My mom rushed over to Carmen.

"How was the flight, mi amor?"

"Good, madrina. Thanks."

My mom turned to Carmen's dad, Uncle Frank, who was not really my uncle but we called him Uncle because his wife was my mom's best friend. My mom gave Uncle Frank a kiss on each cheek and held both of his hands.

"You doing okay?"

Uncle Frank managed a sad sort of smile that reminded me why they were here.

"There're good days and bad days," Uncle Frank offered. "Cari, I can't thank you enough for letting us stay for the summer."

"Cristina was my best friend, Frank. You are family to me."

My mom saw me standing by the lounge and looked annoyed that I hadn't come over to greet them yet.

"Arturo, saluda a tu familia."

The last time I'd seen Carmen, we'd been just kids. My mom and dad had gone to visit them about six months ago for Carmen's mom's funeral, but I was in school, so I couldn't go.

"¡Arturito!" Uncle Frank said. "Cómo ha crecido, Cari." My mom's name is Caridad, but everyone calls her Cari.

I turned to him and smiled. "Thanks. I guess I have grown a little."

"You remember Carmen?" My mom pushed Carmen in front of me.

This was not the lanky, mutant-fast cheetah girl I used

to play tag with years ago. Carmen had changed. She was still tall, but those colorful braces made her look way mature. Her hair was really long and wavy. She carried a little book in her hand, thumbing the edges while looking at me shyly. Then, without warning, she grabbed my shoulders and double kissed me, one on each cheek. I felt a burning in my stomach, like a pot of oil was slowly starting to bubble inside. It. Was. Weird.

"Hola, Arturo," she said.

For a second I considered bolting into the kitchen to try to figure out why I was losing it in front of my mom's goddaughter. I'd better calm down, because Carmen would be living in our apartment complex for the whole summer and possibly beyond. Plus, she was practically my cousin, and these feelings were totally wrong. I didn't know what to do, and if it weren't for Aunt Tuti, I might have been caught in a vortex of my own confusion and despair.

"Hi, Frank. I'm so sorry to hear about everything." Aunt Tuti hugged and double kissed Uncle Frank and then turned to hug Carmen and stroke her hair.

"Ay, she's so beautiful, Frank. Que Dios la bendiga."

"Gracias, Tuti."

"Cari, did you tell them?"

"They just got here, Tuti. How could I have told them?"

"Ay, don't get pesada. I'm trying to pay you a compliment."

"Thank you, Tuti," my mom said as she rolled her eyes.

"Anyway, we are expanding the restaurant!"

"It's not certain yet, Tuti."

"The expansion will be approved, Cari. There's no way the city would reject a good business decision like this."

"That's great," Uncle Frank said.

My mom smiled. "The city put out a call for proposals for the the empty lot next to us—"

Aunt Tuti jumped in before my mom could finish. "And my sister here had the brilliant idea of putting in a bid to expand La Cocina!"

"Fantastic!" Uncle Frank replied.

"Right? This place is barely big enough for our family. Imagine how many more people we could feed with a bigger space. It's the perfect time, because our lease is up at the end of the month." My aunt Tuti paused for a second to take a quick breath before starting up again. She looked like an ostrich the way she moved her really long neck and stuck out her plump, round bottom. "Oye, Frank, maybe you can help with the construction phase?"

Uncle Frank had an eco-friendly construction company in Spain and had built a ton of buildings in Madrid.

"Tuti, Frank has only been here for five minutes. Let's not put him to work already."

"I'm trying to make him feel welcome, Cari. He's been through so much."

Aunt Tuti took out a napkin and began patting her eyes.

"Tuti," my mom started, "please don't get hysterical."

Telling my aunt Tuti not to get hysterical is like telling her, "Please, I want you to totally freak out right now."

"Cari! This is not a time to be calm! He lost his wife!" Aunt Tuti sobbed all the way to the patio, where she joined Mari and Yolanda.

My mom shook her head in frustration and then turned around to address the rest of the family.

"Everyone, we're eating in ten minutes," she said, and then walked Uncle Frank and Carmen to see Abuela before disappearing into the kitchen. Everyone slowly pushed the smaller tables together to make one long table spanning the entire width of the restaurant. A few people grumbled because they knew once the meal was over, they were going to have to start cleaning the restaurant for service the next day.

My mom needed help bringing out the food, so she asked me to go to the patio to call Mari, Yolanda, and Aunt Tuti. I caught them complaining about the humidity outside and in the same breath whining that the air-conditioning was too cold inside. I really didn't understand the women in my family.

As I turned to walk back into the restaurant, I nearly crashed into Carmen, who had appeared out of nowhere.

"Geez!" I said, holding my chest. "You scared me."

"Sorry," she said, smiling. "So, the proposal is to expand the restaurant over there?" Carmen pointed beyond our small patio. The lot was visible from where we stood, with only five small tables and a green awning in our way.

"Huh? Oh, yeah. That whole area," I said, gesturing.

Carmen walked over to the edge of the patio and looked out. I followed her and took in the mostly dark lot that was illuminated by one streetlamp on the far corner.

"Hey," Carmen said, interrupting the silence. "Do you remember when you all came to visit us in Marbella that one summer?"

"Yeah," I said. "What were we? Like, eight?"

"Yeah. I remember you threw sand at me and then tried to run away, but I chased you down the beach."

"And you caught up to me, pinned me to the ground, and dripped wet sand on my back that slithered down my butt when I got up." Oh God. Why did I say that?

Carmen laughed.

"You looked so funny, trying to wash your butt in the water!"

"That water was freezing!"

"Oh, come on," she said. "It wasn't that cold."

"Seawater in southern Spain is *way* colder than the ocean in Miami."

Carmen laughed again. "You never caught me," she said.

"That's because you were, like, a mutant half-cheetah."

I stopped talking when I noticed a figure crossing the street. I don't think Carmen saw it, because she was pointing to the other small buildings lining the neighborhood.

"It's so nice how the buildings are all the same size," she said.

"Yeah," I said, still looking at the figure standing in the shadows.

"Hey, do you see that over there?" I asked.

Carmen followed my gaze.

"Yeah," she said. "It looks like that person is taking something out of a bag. What is it?"

"I don't know."

A couple of quick flashes popped from the mysterious figure.

"They're taking photographs."

"Hey! Hey, you!" Carmen blurted out.

The person looked up from the camera and stared at us. I couldn't see his or her face because it was covered by a large hat. The person put the camera away, walked across the street, and disappeared into the darkness.

"That was weird," Carmen said.

"Yeah," I replied, wondering who would want to take pictures this late at night. But then my mom called us in to eat and we went back inside the restaurant.

Everyone raced to find a seat like they were playing musical chairs or something. They pushed and shoved and complained that they didn't have enough room. But we all settled down once Abuela stood next to her cushioned chair at the head of the table. I arrived at her side because that was always my place. I'm not sure if abuelas are allowed to have favorite grandkids, but I can tell you this: *my* abuela always wanted me to sit next to her.

She motioned for everyone to quiet down. We all joined hands, and when Abuela bowed her head, everyone followed. As she prayed quietly, we were silent. I admit I peeked to my left to see what Carmen was doing— I had a clear shot of her because Vanessa's head was down. Carmen was deep in prayer, mumbling softly to herself.

When Abuela lifted her head to indicate she was finished praying, she caught me looking over at Carmen. Her face lit up when she saw Carmen had just opened her eyes and was looking back at me. My gaze shifted from Abuela to Carmen, and suddenly my cheeks burned and I had trouble breathing. Thankfully, people started to lift their heads, waiting for further instruction from Abuela. She smiled and made the sign of the cross. Everyone did the same—even Mop, and he's Jewish.

With the praying portion of the evening over, nobody waited to be served. Elbows flew as everyone scooped the mushy rice and black beans topped with avocado picked from the tree in our courtyard. They loaded fricasé de pollo from chafing dishes and platters like it was their last meal on earth.

My mom brought Abuela her soup with all the chunks pureed out of it.

"¿Le ayudo, Mami?"

Abuela declined my mom's help and motioned for her to leave the bowl. I noticed Mop trying to get a spoonful of congris, but he couldn't get to the ladle in time. People kept taking it.

Mop's name was actually Benjamin, but we'd nicknamed him Mop because he was skinny and had really shaggy hair. One time we'd been seeing who could stand on their head the longest, and when it had been Mop's turn, Bren had said he looked like a mop cleaning the floor. We'd all laughed, and Mop had decided that he would "henceforth be known as Mop, because I shall clean the earth of all its inequities!" Mop always talked like that. He is definitely my smartest friend.

When dinner ended, we cleaned up and prepared the restaurant for the next day. No one complained as Abuela watched. My family argued a lot, but Abuela always found a way to get everybody on the same page. Mop's and Bren's parents picked them up, and the rest of my family left at different times. I stayed behind with my mom, my dad, Uncle Frank, and Carmen to lock up.

The walk from the restaurant to our apartment complex was about ten minutes. Carmen trailed behind with me as my parents and Uncle Frank walked ahead.

"It must be cool to live in the same building as your whole family," Carmen said. "You always have someone to talk to."

Not only did my entire family work together at La Cocina, but we also lived in the same apartment complex. There was a Zamora in every unit, and this summer Carmen and Uncle Frank were going to live there too.

"Yeah, I guess so," I said. "I like that Abuela is just downstairs, but I'm not sure I like Martín and Brian invading my space all the time."

"I feel kind of lonely back home. That's why I loved when your family came to visit," Carmen said. "Do you remember when we tried to be an eight-foot giant, and we put on my mom's winter coat and you sat on my shoulders while we tried to walk around?" Carmen spoke like the words were at the tip of her tongue at all times.

"I'm pretty sure you got on *my* shoulders," I said, remembering her parents' house in Madrid that same summer we'd gone to the beach.

"You couldn't carry me, remember? We kept falling down."

"Oh, yeah," I said. How embarrassing.

"And then you got on my shoulders, but you didn't

notice the door and you banged your head and we both crashed to the floor!" Carmen laughed.

"That's right," I said, wishing she didn't have such a good memory. We had knocked down a vase of flowers. I remembered how Carmen's mom had come into the room and laughed, watching us in a tangled peacoat covered in fresh floribundas and water. Then my mom walked in, an angry look on her face, but Carmen's mom just put her arm around my mom's shoulders and smiled.

"That was a fun trip," I said. "So, you're just staying in Miami for the summer?"

"Yes. Madrina said it would be good to be with family."

"Yeah. Sorry about, you know, your mom."

"Un día a la vez," she said, and offered a small smile.

"That's what Abuela says." Every time I get frustrated or impatient about something, Abuela reminds me to take it one day at a time.

"It was nice to see you again, Arturo," Carmen said. She turned to follow Uncle Frank into their unit.

"You too," I said. As I walked to my room, I tried to make sense of what had happened tonight. Carmen = Mom's goddaughter/niece was not computing with Arturo + Carmen = sudden frying of intestines when I talked to her.

2

death by soap monsters

I WOKE UP the next morning to the sound of my Hulk alarm blasting "Hulk smash!" in my ear. My first thought—right after *This thing is way too loud*—was about dinner last night. Why had I acted so weird around Carmen? It was probably nothing. I was just excited to see an old friend, or something.

Anyway, I was pumped about starting work at the restaurant. The money I made over the summer was always enough for plenty of movies on the weekends, a new basketball, at least one new pair of kicks, and a whole school year's worth of weekend ice cream trips to Two Scoops, conveniently located around the corner from La Cocina de la Isla.

My mom and dad had already left to buy the morning vegetables for the day's menu. They saved me some tortilla española in a pie pan on the counter. Tortilla española is a great breakfast meal. It's perfect at any temperature, and the egg, onion, and potato fill you up after one slice. I shoveled a whole piece into my mouth, grabbed my keys, and started walking to the restaurant.

I had proven myself last summer when I was the second assistant junior lunch reservations phone operator. That job was cool because I was on the phone all day and got to sit in a really comfortable office chair. More than once I was told I had a really nice speaking voice.

I turned the corner from our apartment complex and walked a few blocks to the main strip, where all the restaurants and shops in Canal Grove were located. And there it was: our colorful sign. The *o* in *Cocina* was bright orange while the rest of the letters were outlined in green and black, and behind the letters was the faint shape of an island. Two multicolored giraffes greeted customers at the entrance of the restaurant, making an arch as you walked through the French double doors. Giraffes were Abuela's favorite animal. I liked them because they were tall and lanky and had big eyes that always looked happy. Like Abuela.

Yolanda was already inside, unfolding chairs while

Mari rolled up forks, knives, and spoons inside napkins. Color defined La Cocina de la Isla. Every bright hue imaginable covered every inch of the interior. Green. Orange. Yellow. Teal. La Cocina was cheerful. It had been like that since Abuela had first opened it nineteen years ago.

My dad had had the walls repainted recently, and even though the paint had already faded a little, it still looked vibrant and fresh. Out back there was a little courtyard with stone columns and an ancient-looking coral stage that was part of the building structure. In that courtyard we hosted countless weddings, birthdays, engagements, anniversaries, and every other kind of party you could imagine.

The hallways leading to the kitchen were covered in picture frames. There was a young Abuela sitting at one of the tables with a US senator and his wife, and another picture where she was sitting with the famous musician Celia Cruz. One where she was being hugged by Gloria and Emilio Estefan. She had taken dozens of photos with telenovela actors, local newscasters, and writers who'd passed through town.

One of my favorite photos was of my mom and Abuela smiling as Abuela symbolically handed my mom a ladle when she took over as head chef. Another picture showed my mom accepting her first major cooking award, the Newbie Chef Challenge competition on the

Food Is Life network. Next to that, a picture of my first basketball team, the Islanders. Abuela bought jerseys for all the players on the team. She'd done that for every one of my sports teams since I was five.

There was a picture of Vanessa accepting the outstanding community citizen award—the youngest person to ever win it. Mari and Yolanda dressed in their prom outfits after they'd decided they would be each other's dates. A large wedding photo of my parents. There was one of Aunt Tuti, my mom, and Uncle Carlos as kids with Abuela and Abuelo at the beach. Compare that to the one of me and all my cousins huddled around Abuela when we were really small. Vanessa and I were cuddled in Abuela's arms.

Everything about La Cocina came back to family. I think that's why so many customers loved it. When they came here, they felt like family too. That was how Abuela wanted it.

I approached the office and waited for my mom to finish her phone call so she could tell me what job I would have. When she hung up, she reached over to a rack and pulled a white chef coat off a hanger.

"What's my job, Mom?" I asked, suddenly excited that she wanted me to be a line cook or something.

"You're going to be the junior lunchtime dishwasher."

The air escaped my lungs.

"Huh?" is all I could muster.

"Didn't you say that you wanted to work in the kitchen this year?" she asked.

"Well, yes, but I was thinking something else, you know? Like a prep cook or something."

"Dishwasher is probably the most important job in the kitchen, Arturo. If dishes aren't clean, we can't serve our customers."

Junior lunchtime dishwasher? It was the worst job ever. I wasn't happy, but I didn't show it. My mother was a no-nonsense chef and boss. Her cooks were respectfully terrified of her. As a dishwasher, I was at the very bottom of the kitchen hierarchy, so I needed to follow the rules and not mess up. Besides, I just had to work three dishwashing shifts a week. What was the worst that could happen?

As soon as I entered the kitchen, Martín threw an apron at me.

"You're late!"

I looked at the clock. It was one minute after nine. Martín followed my eyes and pointed to the clock.

"That clock is not your friend. I. Am not your friend. I. Am your boss. You. Are expected to be here at nine o'clock. I. Better see you here at eight fifty-five. At least! Five minutes before your shift. Not one minute after your shift. Understand? Understand!"

Martín smelled like fried croquetas and a heavy helping of Mira Bro deodorant. I turned my face away.

"Aurelio is out sick today, so you've been promoted from junior dishwasher to assistant prep kitchen dishwasher. Think you can handle it?"

I nodded and put on the apron. I practically lived at my family's restaurant, but being here at this moment in this role felt different. My mom was the chef, but nobody was going to give me special treatment. Especially not Martín.

"What are you scanning around for? Nobody's here to protect you. You might be the favorite out there, but in this kitchen, you're mine!" Could he read minds now?!

He shoved me over to the large dishwashing machine in the corner. There were more levers, buttons, and gauges than the mission control center at NASA. The thing looked like it could transform into a towering sixty-foot robot at any minute. I guess I had never bothered to pay attention to the dishwasher before. It's funny how you can know a place so well and still discover something new and slightly terrifying about it.

"This. Is El Monstruo. Mess with it. And it will eat you. Pull this lever. Press this button. Wait for the cycle to finish. The rack spits out. The dirty water drains. More blue water fills up the tray. Slide another rack into the blue cleaning soap. Dry the rack that comes out. Put it on this dolly. When the dolly is stacked with racks, roll it out and give it to the busboy. The busboy distributes everything to the restaurant. You do it all over again. Think you can handle that, Churroso?"

"Churroso" meant "filthy one." Like he should talk. Martín looked like Jabba the Hutt wearing a chef coat. He pressed a button, and El Monstruo vibrated to life, hissing angrily like we'd woken it up from a nice nap.

The first rack of greasy pots and pans slid onto the table, and the dishwasher let out hisses of steam as the rack splashed into the pool of blue water. The plates kept piling up, and within minutes the glass racks were out of control. I inspected the slimy disaster that was my workstation. After about five or six plates, the blue water looked more like a zombie made out of food bits, preparing to rise up and strangle me in a soggy coil of old grease, chewed-up fried egg, and tomate criollo. Dirty water covered my face.

Martín returned, carrying a tower of filthy frying pans. By the time I turned around, he was already tossing them into the air.

"Uno. Dos. Tres. Cuatro. Cinco!" Martín said, flinging each one like a Frisbee. I didn't have time to react, so each pan torpedoed into the blue water and, like a depth charge, held on for a moment before blowing up in my face.

I tried to cover my Miami Heat shirt by shielding myself, but it was no use. The apron protected nothing. I was soaked.

"¡Ah, pobrecito!" cracked Martín. "Did Churroso ruin his little basketball tee-tee? Serves you right for working too slow!"

I looked at the clock. I wasn't going to let El Monstruo beat me. I focused on the incoming racks and moved them through the newly filled blue water and into the machine. I pulled the lever and pressed the button and dried the first rack, then the next and the next. Soon the dolly filled up.

Martín glanced over and scoffed, pointing to a tiny speck on one of the plates.

"Do you think our customers are going to like grime with their plantain mash, Churroso?"

I shook my head, frustrated but determined not to let Jabba the Chef get to me.

"Clean this one again."

He shoved the plate into my chest and made me hand-wash it in front of him. He crossed his arms and waited as I tried to rub the tiny speck off the plate.

"More," he said. "I want to see my face in it."

I could hear him breathing heavily, and the mix of food and really strong deodorant was making me nauseous. The little spot finally came off, and I handed the plate back to him.

He inspected it and then walked back to his station to continue prepping for lunch.

"Get back to work," he said, and mumbled something about me under his breath.

The other racks continued to pile up. The restaurant hadn't even opened yet, and I needed to wash more than twenty racks!

I found out later that the pots and pans got a steam in El Monstruo and then were cleaned with olive oil before the restaurant opened, because cast iron is dense and takes time to heat up. The steam started the job, and then the heat from the stove tops did the rest. The plates and glasses got steamed to remove any spots or grime left from the night before. Aurelio, the regular dishwasher, did this every morning, but today the job had fallen to me and it was brutal. By the time I finished with the early morning dish prep, I had practically drowned in soap bubbles.

I hung up my apron and looked out at the dining room to find that Abuela had arrived. The restaurant had just opened, but customers were already waving her over, dying for some one-on-one time with their old friend.

She sat at a table with a group of ladies. Even though she was older, she hardly ever slouched. Abuela always dressed like she was on her way to a fancy party. She either wore lots of jewelry—always her shiny silver necklace with cross and oval pendant—or silky scarves with colorful prints. I once bought her a scarf with giraffes on it for her birthday. She said it was her absolute favorite scarf of all time.

Customers accepted her friendly kisses. She admired the necklace of one of the women at the table, taking it in her hands. The lady's name was Martha, and she owned a jewelry shop a few stores down from La Cocina. She was a lunch regular. Abuela got up and lovingly rubbed Martha's shoulder before going to another table.

Abuela took small steps toward a group having a business lunch, and they immediately stopped their serious discussion to speak with her. One of the men got up from his chair and offered it to Abuela while a lady in a suit moved over excitedly to make room. They were a group of lawyers from Cohen, Carr & Crespo—a law firm at the far end of Main Street. Every Monday, without fail, they walked in rain, heat, or humidity to La Cocina to have lunch and get their week started.

Abuela never stayed at a table too long. Sometimes she cleared a plate or refilled water glasses. We had twenty tables in the restaurant, and it was always packed. There was hardly room to move around when it was completely full, but Abuela always made her way to every single table.

Aunt Tuti rushed over to help her, but Abuela politely brushed her youngest daughter away. Aunt Tuti shook her head nervously as she walked back to the hostess stand, mumbling before seating another guest.

Behind me, the kitchen doors swung open, and my mom walked through, wearing her signature uniform: a bright-orange chef coat with *Cari* in fancy cursive on the upper left side. She had a La Cocina baseball cap on her head and a newspaper under her arm.

"How was your first day?" my mom asked, stopping in front of me.

"Good. Except the dishwasher almost ate me."

She laughed and was about to turn into the office when she saw Abuela.

"When did Abuela get here?"

"She was already here when I finished my shift."

My mom went over to Aunt Tuti at the hostess stand. Aunt Tuti started flailing her arms, and my mom kept shaking her head while watching Abuela happily chat with a couple. I recognized them because they'd had their engagement party at La Cocina a couple of months ago. Their names were Annabelle and George.

My mom walked over to the couple, said hello, and then turned to walk away, smiling uncomfortably as she tried to get Abuela to follow her. I noticed how differently people reacted when they saw my mom in the dining room. They whispered and looked at each other the way people do when they see a celebrity. I guess being on a famous reality TV show kind of makes you a celebrity.

Abuela held Annabelle's and George's hands as she said good-bye. She followed my mom to the kitchen but insisted on talking to everyone on the way.

They approached, and Abuela's face lit up when she

saw me. I reached out for a hug. Even though I was already taller than Abuela, she still made me feel as little as when she'd read stories to me when I was younger.

My favorite was *El Ratón Pérez*, about a mouse that fell into a pot of soup. Abuela did voices, and at the end of this and every story she'd say, "¡Y colorín, colorado, este cuento se ha acabado!" Now most days, I read to her.

My mom waited impatiently for Abuela. It seemed like Abuela enjoyed how uncomfortable my mom was, because she kept introducing her to guests. My mom and Abuela loved each other so much, but there was always this kind of friction between them because they were so different. While they were next to each other like this, the differences were pretty obvious—they looked like total opposites. Abuela was tall and slender, and my mom was much shorter and had powerful hands and a strong build.

I turned back to the dining room, which was totally full. Aunt Tuti talked to people as they waited to be seated. Mari and Yolanda served tables while other friends and family bussed or ran food or prepared drinks for guests.

The front door opened, and a man dressed in a crisp white suit and a wide-brimmed hat walked in. He took off his hat as soon as he entered, and then smiled brightly at Aunt Tuti. Aunt Tuti moved around the hostess stand to greet him, and the man took her hand and kissed it. She turned around, and I could see that she was blushing.

The man took a menu from Aunt Tuti and walked toward the bar. He smiled and very politely bowed and said hello to everyone who made eye contact with him. Abuela watched the man cross the dining room and take a seat on one of the barstools. He tipped his head to Abuela. She smiled, but not in her usual warm way. My mom was still trying to get Abuela out of the dining room, so I don't think she noticed the man.

Abuela walked over, and as soon as she got near, the man stood up and took her hand. He went to kiss it, but she took it back before he could. It didn't seem like she wanted to accept such a gesture from someone she clearly didn't know.

"Doña Veronica," the man said to Abuela.

"¿Sí?" Abuela responded.

"Soy Wilfrido Pipo," he said, showing off a mouth full of perfect white teeth. "I just opened an office a few blocks away."

"Bienvenido, Wilfrido," Abuela responded.

"Gracias," he said.

There was something off about the way Abuela had said, "Welcome." Like maybe she didn't really mean it. My mom took Abuela's arm once again, and they came back to the kitchen. When they got to me, Abuela let go of my mom and took my hand.

"Vamos a la casa, Arturito," she said. "Estoy un poco cansada."

Abuela told me she was tired as she looked back at the impeccably dressed man. I left the restaurant with her, but not before hearing the man compliment the menu. I wondered what kind of business he had opened up. When I asked Abuela, she said she didn't know.

"No sé quién es, mi amor," she said.

While we walked, she quietly sang a song she used to sing to me when I was a kid. "Guantanamera. Guajira, guantanamera . . . Yo soy un hombre sincero, de donde crece la palma. . . ."

I opened the gate to our apartment complex and walked Abuela to her unit on the first floor. She said she was pretty tired, so I helped her to her recliner. She closed her eyes almost immediately. I tried calling Mop and Bren. They weren't answering their phones, so I decided to get the mail and deliver it to each apartment. I had the master key because another one of my summer jobs was assistant apprentice super for my family's complex. I'd started digging through the mail when someone came up from behind and startled the frijoles out of me.

3

chicken pot poems

ENVELOPES SCATTERED ALL over the place as I jumped back.

"I'm sorry—I didn't mean to scare you!"

It was Carmen.

"Hey, what's up, Carmen?"

Maybe my greeting was a little too enthusiastic, because she got all wide-eyed like she couldn't understand why I was yelling so loud. I guess maybe I was happy to see her. I dunno—it was strange.

"Hey right back!" Her face lit up, and her smile practically went from ear to ear. In the bright sun, the freckles on her cheeks were really noticeable. Like cinnamon sprinkles. I wasn't exactly sure what to say to her.

"Um, are you hot?" I asked. "I mean not hot like *hot*, but like sweating hotness . . . from the heat and, um, you're in Miami."

"I am," she said. "And it *is* hot. It feels like Zimbabwe in August." She put the book she was holding onto the mailbox and then pulled her reddish-brown hair into a ponytail.

"Yeah," I said, not exactly sure where Zimbabwe was.

The look on my face must have told her as much, because she said, "It's in southern Africa. The climate is really similar to Miami, except Zimbabwe is landlocked."

"Right, that makes sense. So, what are you reading?"

"It's José Martí's *Versos sencillos*. I have to finish it for school next year."

"That sounds painful."

"I love poetry, actually. I really admire poets who can bare their souls on the page, you know?"

"I . . . like poetry?"

"Is that a question?"

"No, I mean, I don't . . . I mean, not really, um, poetry. I write it . . . sometimes."

It was a horrible, shameless lie. I had never written a poem in my life.

"Cool," she said. "Maybe I can read it sometime."

"Yeah, sure, why not?" Why, why did I tell her this?

Carmen laughed, her skin flushed. She fanned herself with her hand.

"When I'm in the sun too long," she said, "I look like a lobster tail that's just been pulled out of a pot of boiling water."

I knew just what she meant.

"I get really pink," I said. "Like salmon-in-an-oven-too-long pink."

"I can see that."

"Huh?"

"So," she said, interrupting my total awkwardness. "How was your first day at work? Did you get to answer phones again like you wanted?"

"Nope. I cleaned pots and dishes all day and ended up covered in soap bubbles. And I almost got eaten by the gigantic dishwasher."

"Wow, that stinks," Carmen said, chuckling a little. "I mean, I guess *you* don't stink 'cause, you know, the soap bubbles."

"Right!" I said. "Because soap bubbles are clean, and why would I stink if I were drenched in soap?" Wow, way to state the obvious.

Carmen smiled and helped me sort through the mail.

"Abuela invited me to come to the restaurant with her, but I couldn't because my dad wants me to study in the mornings."

"Yeah, she stopped by to say hi to everyone like she

always does. Some strange guy came into the restaurant, acting like he knew everybody. Abuela didn't seem to like him very much."

"Wow," Carmen offered. "Abuela likes everyone."

It was true. "La gente le gusta hablar de sus cosas," she always told me.

Over the years I realized how true that was. People really did like talking about themselves. Whether it was about a wedding or a new baby or a kid who got accepted into a great college or a family member who had passed away, Abuela was always there to listen. When customers returned, Abuela recalled details of specific conversations easily. It made the regulars feel loved. If a new customer walked in, Abuela made it a point to learn a little about them. If customers didn't want to talk or share anything, Abuela would leave them alone but would always shake their hands and thank them for eating at the restaurant. I never saw anybody leave La Cocina de la Isla without a smile. This new guy was the only customer I'd seen Abuela treat differently.

Carmen stared at me, and I realized it was because I hadn't said anything in a really long time.

"Arturo? You okay?"

"Huh? Yeah, sorry."

I glanced awkwardly at my phone and saw Mop had texted me. He told me to meet him and Bren at the basketball courts.

"Um, I gotta go, so I guess I'll, um, see you around," I said, because I didn't really want her to play ball with Mop and Bren. I knew what they'd say, and I didn't feel like explaining why I was suddenly so interested in having a girl around, even though that girl was super-cool . . . but also my mom's goddaughter. I just needed to shut up and get the heck out of there. Before I could do anything, though, Carmen gave me a kiss on each cheek and turned to leave.

"See you later, alligator," she said, which left me half-frozen long enough to notice that she had left her book of poems on the mailbox.

4

ice scream: a dialogue

*BREN AND MOP are in the middle of tossing free throws
when I get to the court. A huge dark cloud rolls in, threat-
ening to rain on our game. It rains almost every afternoon
in the summer.*

BREN: Dude, what's in your hand?

ME: Um, a book.

BREN: What kind of book?

ME: A book of poems.

Bren stops dribbling.

BREN: By poems, you mean, like, rap lyrics?

Mop interrupts us and takes the book out of my hand.

MOP: José Martí? Cool. Didn't know you were reading that.

ME: Um, I'm not. I mean, I guess I could—will—maybe read it.

BREN: I don't know any rappers named José. Is he new?

MOP: Bren. Martí was a revolutionary hero in the Cuban War for Independence against Spain in the late 1800s.

BREN: A Cuban rapper from the 1800s? Dude, that's awesome.

Bren tries to shoot a three but airballs.

MOP: Are you sure you want to try out for the eighth-grade team?

BREN: I have a chance to start.

Mop and I look at each other.

BREN: So, Arturo, perchance does that book of Cuban rapper poems belong to a special someone who popped into your life the other day after so many years apart?

ME: What? No.

Bren stops shooting and smiles.

BREN: Bro, she was, like, the tallest girl I've ever seen. She's almost your height, Arturo.

Mop takes the ball from Bren.

MOP: Every time you say *bro*, the English language loses its will to live.

BREN: Dude, I think you should totally ask her out.

ME: No way. My mom is her godmother! We're practically related. Can we just play?

Mop and Bren look at each other, then back at me.

BREN: I think someone's got a thing for his godsister.

ME: No, I don't. And there's no such thing as a godsister.

Bren eyes the book in my hand.

BREN: Then why are you reading her book of Cuban love poems?

ME: She left it behind. I just need to return it to her.

Rain starts coming down in little drops, but the sun is still out. Mop takes one last shot, which banks in while Bren looks at me funny.

BREN: Dude, I can loan you my Pitbull imitation shades. Those are killer.

MOP: What does that have to do with Arturo reading poetry, Bren?

BREN: Because the shades will make him look cool. And tall girls like guys who are cool.

Mop slaps his forehead as we walk off the courts.

MOP: Dude, I wish I didn't have to leave for camp this week.

BREN: Me too! Man, I wish I weren't going away! I feel it's my duty to teach Arturo Cuban hip-hop.

MOP: You're from Northampton, Massachusetts, Bren. Not Cuba.

We leave the courts and start down the alley and onto Main Street.

ME: Guys, seriously. I'm not interested in Carmen

like that. I mean, she's cool and all, but we're practically related.

BREN: Hey, bro, when love calls, love calls.

ME: Can we stop talking about it? Let's just go get ice cream.

MOP: An excellent idea!

We walk to Two Scoops and take in the sights of summer. Long humid days turn into showery afternoons. And pink sunsets conclude each day like the swirl of a mango, guava, and papaya sorbet. It doesn't get dark until about eight o'clock. Sometimes nine.

We eat our cones quickly, careful not to drip melted ice cream onto our clothes. I look across the street and notice a fancy sign with cursive writing on it above a new store. I can't read the sign until I get really close. It says: PIPO PLACE—THE FUTURE IS NOW.

ME: Guys, this weird man came into La Cocina today and told us he'd just opened a place few blocks from the restaurant. I wonder if this is it.

Mop examines the storefront from across the street.

MOP: It looks like it could be a boutique clothing shop. The sign looks flashy.

BREN: Bro, that would be awesome if it is. I need to get some fly clothes before school starts. Can't roll into eighth grade wearing these rags.

MOP: Bren, if your clothes get any brighter, the sun is going to cease to rise.

ME: You will literally cause the next ice age.

BREN: Don't hate the flavor, fellas. El sabor Latino.

MOP: We're trying to save humanity from your wardrobe.

BREN: Come on—let's go to my house and play Legends of the Universe.

MOP: Finally a good idea comes out of the man's mouth!

We walk and talk and each take turns dribbling our ball through the neighborhood. The rest of the week is exactly what I want out of summer. I hang out with Mop and Bren every day after my shifts at the restaurant, I see Carmen occasionally around the apartment complex, and I eat a ton of ice cream. Life is good until Sunday family dinner when disaster strikes.

5

conspiracy theories

AUNT TUTI WAS making it really hard for us to prep for Sunday family dinner.

"Cari, did you read the paper today?" she asked my mom. "I can't believe there's another bid for the lot next door! Did you tell Mami?"

"Yes, I read it. And, no, I don't want to worry her."

I watched Aunt Tuti pace nervously around the dining room at the restaurant while making a face like she was about to swallow an entire apple.

"*Every day* this week!" she yelled at the top of her lungs. "He's stopped by the restaurant *every day*. He even invited me to lunch. Can you believe it? He. Invited me. To lunch. Engreído. Mentiroso. Ah no, no way. No way!"

"Tuti, cálmate. You're getting hysterical."

Hearing that word sent Tuti off again.

"Hysterical? *Hys. Ter. Ical?* Am I the only one who cares about this family?"

"Oh my God, there she goes again." My uncle Carlos slapped his forehead and went to the kitchen to grab a pitcher of water for the table. We were almost ready to sit down to dinner.

"¿Qué pasa?" Abuela asked from the other side of the room as Aunt Tuti flailed her arms around like she was painting the air.

"Nada, Mami," my mom replied, then turned to Aunt Tuti. "Tuti, you're making Mami nervous; you need to sit down. We'll discuss this at the table."

"Fine. But it needs to be addressed."

"I know. Just sit down, please."

"Dang, she gets so hyster—"

"Don't say that!" the family yelled out before Brian could finish.

Carmen couldn't help but giggle. "Let's both yell *hysterical* at the same time and see what she does."

"That could be really dangerous," I said. "There's a ton of people in here, and Aunt Tuti likes using her hands a lot."

Aunt Tuti shook her head while my cousins tried to get her to calm down.

"Who else put a bid in, Mom?" I finally asked.

"You don't need to concern yourself with it, Arturo. Go and wash up. We're eating in ten minutes."

My mom put the newspaper on the hostess stand and went back into the kitchen to finish prepping. Before I left to wash up, I glanced at the paper and saw what Aunt Tuti was talking about.

"What does it mean?" Carmen asked behind me.

"It means La Cocina de la Isla isn't the only business that wants to build on the lot next to the restaurant."

"Who else wants to build there?"

I showed the paper to Carmen. On the cover was a photo of the man in the white suit. He was holding up a sign with the same fancy lettering as the store I'd seen earlier. The words PIPO PLACE were written in tacky gold cursive.

"We've been around for nineteen years! No one deserves to expand more than us!" Aunt Tuti yelled, trying to make eye contact with anyone who would listen. "Ay, I can't believe I let him kiss my hand! I feel disgusting."

"Tuti, if we don't win the bid, we'll just have a new neighbor. That's all."

My dad, Uncle Carlos, Martín, and Brian moved our tables toward the center of the restaurant to make one long table. Bren and Mop tried to help, but Bren somehow fell under a table and Martín (aka Jabba the Chef) stepped on him.

"So Arturo's little friends help out, but Churroso just stands there, watching?"

"I'm helping Abuela," I told him.

"Must be nice," Martín taunted. "Must. Be. Nice."

Martín was such a hater. I shook my head and went to wash my hands. When I came out of the bathroom, I saw Carmen looking at the pictures on the wall. She smiled at the one of nine-year-old me standing alone holding a basketball against my hip. My jersey was so big, it looked like I was wearing a dress.

"I played on the eleven-to-thirteen-year-old team, and that was the smallest jersey they had," I said, now embarrassed that Abuela had put that picture up in the restaurant.

"You've grown a lot since then," Carmen said, and my cheeks suddenly felt like they had really bad sunburn.

Back at the table, Vanessa carefully placed each drinking glass in exactly the same position. She complained that Bren was slamming them on the table too hard.

"He's going to break the glasses, Arturo. Tell him to be careful."

Vanessa was older than us by six months, and she ran in social circles that included girls and guys who were likely to become senators, ambassadors, and Nobel Prize winners.

Bren held the glass in his hand and stared at Vanessa.

"What is that smell?" she asked, wrinkling her nose.

Bren quietly sniffed his armpits. "It's Mira Bro power deodorant."

Mira Bro was a line of really sparkly men's jewelry, tight patterned shirts and jeans, and most famously, a really, really potent men's deodorant. Only two people I knew wore that stuff—Bren and Martín.

My family piled around the large table as my mom brought out food from the kitchen. Vanessa brushed against Bren's shoulder as she stepped around him, which must have made him nervous, because he looked like he could fall face first into the picadillo.

"If you want to impress a girl, Brendan, do it with this," Vanessa said, pointing to his head. "Not with . . . with that." She scrunched her face and held her breath, avoiding any more of the funky deodorant. I quickly glanced at Carmen and we made eye contact. I think I smiled. I can't be sure, because it felt like there was an organ lodged in my throat. So maybe it looked like I was choking instead of smiling.

Almost as soon as Abuela had finished leading prayer, the family started talking about the lot situation again.

"Okay, so what's the plan, Cari?" Uncle Carlos asked.

"Yes, fearless leader, *what* is the plan?" Aunt Tuti challenged.

"The plan," my mom began, "is to go about business as usual."

"What?!"

Questions and complaints fired back and forth across the table.

"What are you talking about, Cari? You want to do nothing?"

"Listen, everyone." My mom stood, her hand on my dad's chair. "We presented our proposal to expand. The city is still going to hold a public forum. Wilfrido Pipo doesn't change that. We are considered favorites because we are the true face of this community. Our neighbors know us and trust us. If we start trying to do something drastic and changing what people love about our place, we'll confuse the community. And then we'll really be in trouble."

My family hurled more complaints across the table like we were playing a really angry game of verbal dodgeball.

"Cari's right."

"Nobody ever accomplished *anything* by doing *nothing*."

"I don't agree. I don't agree."

Everyone turned to Tía Abuela Josephina, who almost never spoke.

"What don't you agree with, Tía?" my mom asked.

"Everything."

Voices erupted, and soon it felt like there was one big noise demon hovering over the dinner table. Then Abuela stood and everyone froze.

"La comida . . . se va a enfriar." It was hard for Abuela

to get the words out, but she still sounded powerful. Aunt Tuti and the rest of the adults looked embarrassed. What followed was the quietest dinner we'd ever had. The only sounds were the clinking of forks and spoons against plates and serving dishes. Occasionally Vanessa would sigh heavily when she'd get an unfortunate whiff of Bren's deodorant. I could tell he was trying not to make any sudden movements so he could contain his smell.

I picked at my picadillo. I rolled the olives and crispy potatoes around with my fork, wondering why my family couldn't agree on the right thing to do about Wilfrido. La Cocina de la Isla had been in my family forever. It was our second home, and we just wanted to share more of it with the town. What could Wilfrido Pipo want with this old lot?

"How do you spell his name?"

Carmen had popped up right next to my face and scared me so much that I accidentally launched a few peas at Martín. (He wasn't pleased.) Mop and Bren had finished eating and gotten up from the table, so Carmen slid into Mop's seat next to me.

"Geez, you have got to stop springing up on me like that!"

"Sorry," Carmen said. She had her phone in hand, ready to type. I looked out to the lot and saw Mop and Bren at the edge of the patio, looking into the restaurant at me. Mop gave a thumbs-up while Bren gyrated and did some weird dance move and almost fell over. I shook my head and ignored them.

"So, let's see what we can find out about Wilfrido," Carmen said, sounding totally pumped up.

"I'd put your phone away if I were you," I warned. "Tía Abuela Josephina will pinch your ear and take it away if she sees it out at the table."

"I'll be care—" Carmen didn't even have time to finish her sentence before Tía Abuela Josephina swooped in, plucked Carmen's phone from her hands, and set it on the serving counter next to the urns of my family members who were here "in spirit."

"I told you so," I said.

"Well, at least she didn't pinch my ear!" Carmen giggled, and the sound made my insides feel like there was a six-pound snapper flopping around in there.

"Hey," I said, shaking off the funny feeling, "maybe we should—"

"Sneak into Wilfrido's house and find out where he's hiding the dead bodies?"

I looked at Carmen, totally confused. "Huh?"

"That's not what you were thinking?" she asked.

"I was thinking we should check out his store."

"That's what I was thinking," Carmen said, and tightened her lips. She looked as though she had eaten something she wasn't sure she liked.

"We'll go and see what kind of store he has. Maybe it

will give us clues about what he plans to do with the lot if he wins."

"What if he's plotting a sinister takeover of Miami and we're the only ones who can stop him?"

"Um . . ."

"Or"—she leaned in close, squinted, and whispered— "what if he's an alien sent down to probe us before the invading army attacks and eats all of our brains?!"

I stared.

"Or," I said, "he wants to expand his business into the lot because it's a popular location?"

"Or that. So," Carmen continued, "what's the plan?"

"We'll go to his place together?"

"Okay. Bring your best disguise," she said, like it was the most normal thing in the world to say.

"Why?" I asked.

"Because we're going sleuthing!"

Carmen jumped into her original seat when Mop came back inside. He gave me a wink and a nudge, and I could feel my cheeks burning. To make matters worse, I looked over at Abuela, and she was watching me with a sly smile. She raised her eyebrows up and down like she was in on a joke I didn't get.

Later that night, after everyone had gone home, I stayed awake in my bed, wondering what on earth Carmen meant about wearing a disguise.

6

cigar box secrets

A FEW DAYS had passed, and we were doing a bad job of going about "business as usual." The vibe at La Cocina de la Isla felt like guacamole that had turned brown and bitter. Aunt Tuti kept mumbling to herself about how much she disliked Wilfrido. Abuela started complaining more frequently about her breathing, and you could tell it was getting harder for her to get around. This had everyone on edge. Martín was in an especially nasty mood today, and I could hear him yelling orders at the cooks. He waddled around like a hippo standing on two feet, and the mixture of highly perfumed deodorant and fried grease was making me queasy. As soon as the lunch shift ended, I took my bag and shoved my dishwasher shirt inside. I still had Carmen's book of poetry in it, and I made a mental note to return it to her. Poetry was definitely *not* in my future.

I bolted out of the restaurant and went home to play video games. But guess who I saw on my way. That's right: Carmen.

"Hey," I said, careful not to sound too excited.

"Hey," she said.

"So, had a nice day?"

"Yeah," she said, "I went to Abuela's house and watched TV with her, but she was coughing a lot, so I just let her rest. Then I went with my dad to the store."

"Cool, thanks for checking on Abuela."

"We're family; that's what we do."

I can't lie—I felt a little deflated when she said that, like cake cooked at the wrong temperature. I don't know why I cared so much, but I didn't want Carmen saying we were related.

Carmen kept talking to fill the silence while I was thinking.

"I like hanging out with Abuela. It's just nice to feel close to people, you know?"

"Yeah," I said, thinking Carmen must really miss her mom.

"It's the same thing when we talk. You and Abuela are both kind souls."

Did she really just compare hanging out with me to

hanging out with someone's grandmother? She sees me like an *abuela*?

I rushed into telling a story so I wouldn't have to think about what Carmen had said anymore. "Abuela used to take me to the beach early in the morning every summer until she got sick."

"Really?"

"Just me and Abuela. She would show up at our door with a bag full of beach toys, already wearing sunscreen, a wide-brimmed straw hat, and really round sunglasses. Sometimes I'd sleep in my swim trunks so I'd be ready first thing."

"How cute! Sounds like fun."

"Yeah. We would get to the beach before anyone else. She'd hold my hand as we picked conch shells out of the shallow water. Then I'd stand on her knees and she'd pretend she was a Jet Ski and twirl me around. I haven't been to the beach in a while."

"My mom and I used to do the Jet Ski thing too," Carmen said.

"How long ago did she get sick?"

"Doesn't matter," she said, and then suddenly changed the subject. "Hey, when do you want to go to Wilfrido Pipo's store? We could try to go tomorrow."

"Yeah, sure. But about the disguises—"

"What about them?" she said, arching her eyebrow.

"Why do we have to dress up again?"

"Because your face will be too recognizable!" she shouted. "Wilfrido has been to La Cocina, and we might not be able to collect as much evidence if he sees you."

"Evidence of what?" I asked.

"Anything, Arturo. It could be anything."

When we got home, I saw Abuela outside, carefully tending to her plants in the courtyard. She dropped soil onto the ground and spread it with the cane she'd started using to help her get around. Carmen ran up to Abuela and gave her a kiss. I grabbed a pair of gloves from Abuela and got onto my hands and knees to help spread the dirt around the base of the floribunda bush.

"It hasn't bloomed at all," I said.

"She just needs a little TLC," Carmen replied.

When I finished patting down the dirt, I took the gloves off and folded them. I wiped the sweat off my face with my arm and accidently smudged a little dirt across my forehead. Abuela handed me a white handkerchief.

Carmen giggled and pointed.

"I think, um, there might be compost on your forehead."

I rubbed it off and stared at it. Great, I'd smudged poop on my face in front of Carmen. Why couldn't I just be cool?!

"Pronto, yo creo," Abuela said, interrupting the awkwardness.

"She keeps thinking they're going to bloom soon," I

said, smearing the compost back onto the grass. "But we've tried everything."

"A little hope never hurt anyone," Carmen said.

Abuela told us about the time Abuelo had made her grilled steak with black beans, and he'd kept overcooking the steak and undercooking the beans. But he'd never stopped trying, she said. I guess watching the flowerless floribunda made Abuela think of Abuelo.

Uncle Frank stepped out of the apartment and called to Carmen. "Can you help me with something, mi amor?"

"Sí, Papi," she said, then turned back to me. "I'll see you later?"

I nodded and kind of waved. Abuela noticed and nudged me forward, encouraging me to say good-bye properly. I gave Carmen a double kiss, which sent my face into a lobster boil.

Now it was just the two of us, and I walked Abuela to her apartment. The first thing she did when she got inside was head to her little kitchen to make a batido from fresh mangos that had fallen from the neighbor's tree. Every summer when the mango trees started giving fruit, the couple who lived in the building next to ours would give her a grocery bag full of ripe, delicious mangos. Abuela would peel a whole stack and freeze them. She'd make them into smoothies for her grandkids and neighbors. I was usually the first to taste one each summer.

We took two plastic cups and savored the sweet, pulpy orange-colored drink. Abuela sat in her recliner, and I took a seat on the couch next to her. I put my bag on the floor, and unzipped it to grab some gum inside. Abuela noticed Carmen's book in the top pocket and before I could cram it farther into the bag, she snatched it up.

She read the cover then she glanced at me. I could barely see her bright eyes through the sea of wrinkles surrounding them. She reached for the reading glasses sitting on top of her head. That was when I noticed how gray her hair had gotten. For as long as I could remember, Abuela's hair had always been brown and tucked into a perfect bun. She always wanted to look her best. But today her hair was a little out of place, and gray strands stuck out in several places. She flipped through the pages and smiled as she quietly read.

"Entonces," she said, finally looking up. "Este libro de poesía, ¿qué hace en tu bolsa, Arturito?"

"Nothing," I said. "It's not my book. It's, um . . . It's a friend's book—I mean, libro."

"Y ese 'friend,' ¿es un *amigo* o una *amiga*?" she asked, smirking.

Abuela was wondering if the "friend" was a certain honey-eyed, wavy-haired girl who was staying in our apartment complex over the summer. I shrugged and tried to act cool.

Luckily, Abuela seemed to drop it. Instead she began

to tell me another story I sort of knew—the time she came to Miami from Cuba.

"Sabía que no iba a regresar," she said quietly, remembering the day she knew she would not return to Cuba.

I knew Abuela had come to Miami on a boat a long time ago. She told that story a lot.

"¿Tú sabes que tu abuelo escribía poesía?" she asked.

"Abuelo wrote poetry?" That, I didn't know.

"Y le encantaba la poesía de José Martí. Como la Carmen."

Abuela explained that Abuelo had loved the same poet who was on the cover of Carmen's book. I think she was trying to make an embarrassing romantic connection.

"¿Tú sabes cómo tu abuelo y yo nos conocimos en Cuba?" Abuela asked.

"No," I said.

Abuela walked over to her bookshelf and took out a large wooden cigar box. Inside the box was a stack of letters neatly tied together with string, a few pens, a watch that didn't work, and a folded envelope.

"Aquí está la historia de tu abuelo y yo," she said, and handed me the dark-brown box that smelled like earth. When I looked at it more closely, I realized it wasn't just a stack of letters—there were also photographs, an old CD, and blank stationery. Abuela looked at me. She pulled the loose strands of her thin gray hair back into a bun. Then she sat down in her recliner and told me to

take the box. The box, she said, was the story of how poetry had helped bring her and Abuelo together.

Abuela squeezed my hand, winked, and smiled.

"Lo más importante, Arturito," she said, "es el amor
y la fe."

Love and faith are most important. What does that
even mean? I tucked Abuelo's box and Carmen's book of
poems into my bag. I kissed Abuela good-bye and walked
to my apartment. That was when I checked Twitter and
saw some DMs from Bren and Mop.

@PITBULL4LIF: wat up, bro!!!

@THEUBIQUITOUSMOP: Hear, hear, good sir.

@PITBULL4LIF: dude, every time i see ur handle,
it weirds me out. what does it mean again???

@THEUBIQUITOUSMOP: It means I am a
ubiquitous mop. I am present and found
everywhere. Cleaning the world.

@PITBULL4LIF: ur so weird, dude.

@THEUBIQUITOUSMOP: Says the guy with a
life-size Pitbull cutout in his room that he talks to
every night.

@PITBULL4LIF: he's my rock, bro. he gives me strength.

@ARTZAM3: Guys, Abuela gave me this cool cigar box from my abuelo.

@THEUBIQUITOUSMOP: Intriguing. What's in it?

@ARTZAM3: A whole bunch of letters, photographs, some blank pages, and a CD.

@THEUBIQUITOUSMOP: Have you read any of the letters?

@ARTZAM3: Not yet. I'm going to get some rest. Carmen wants to go check out Wilfrido Pipo's store tomorrow.

@PITBULL4LIF: dude! let me go with!!! been dying to get my hands on some fresh new threads.

@ARTZAM3: Um, Carmen kind of wanted to do an undercover thing. Just the two of us.

I waited for them to respond. Finally both Mop and Bren's messages popped up at practically the same time.

@PITBULL4LIF: OH YEAH????

@THEUBIQUITOUSMOP: INTERESTING!!!!

@ARTZAM3: Not like that. Good night!

Bren sent a whole bunch of kissing emojis, and Mop joined in with hearts. Very annoying. Carmen and I were just two friends checking out what kind of store Wilfrido Pipo had. Nothing else.

Then Bren gave me advice on what to wear. I had no interest in dressing like a rapper. But that would have been better than what I ended up wearing.

7

masking the stench

THE NEXT DAY, I dug through my clothes for a disguise that would make me unrecognizable to Wilfrido, yet cool to Carmen. Something that made me look like a spy from a Bond film. But I didn't have a tuxedo. And the only pair of sunglasses I could find were my mom's bright orange ones. I tried looking in my dad's closet for something when Carmen knocked at the door. Desperate, I ran back to my room and grabbed some clothes out of a box full of stuff I was going to give to my little cousins. As I slid on my choice of disguise, my arms felt like they were going to burst through the fabric. With no time to second guess, I threw on my sneakers, slid on the accompanying mask, and bolted to the door. When I opened it, my jaw dropped.

"Hey," she said. Thank goodness I had a mask on, because I didn't want Carmen to see how red my cheeks probably were. She wore heels that made her look five inches taller, and makeup that made her look ten years older. Her hair was totally done up, and a pair of glasses completed her disguise. Like I said, she looked way older than thirteen, and I felt like a complete idiot.

"The Hulk! I like the choice," she said. "You could be, like, my little brother or something."

Her little brother? This was a disaster.

"I'll go change," I said through the mask, which made my voice sound like I had a bad case of asthma.

"No! It's perfect," she said, grabbing my arm. "Come on—let's go."

I really wanted to change, but Carmen insisted that it was a great choice for a costume. She said nobody would suspect a kid dressed like a superhero of snooping for information.

The *clack-clack* of Carmen's high heels mixed with my increasingly muffled breathing as we walked down the street. It was a typical summer Miami afternoon where the humidity punishes any and all. Especially idiots who wear superhero costumes that don't fit and rubber masks that only have one small hole to breathe through. Costumes like this should be outlawed from any place where the humidity is greater than 10 percent.

Carmen and I continued down the street in silence. It was really awkward. I lifted my mask because I couldn't bear the heat anymore. I tugged at the fake Hulk muscles squeezing my real chest, and desperately hoped the costume would break and we would have to go back so I could change into regular clothes.

"Wait, put your mask back on," Carmen said. "We're getting close to Wilfrido's store."

I really didn't want to, but Carmen told me it was the only way we were going to find out exactly what was going on.

"If he recognizes you, he might not share information."

I didn't think Wilfrido cared about a couple of kids checking out his store, but I went with it anyway. As soon as I put my mask back on, I felt sweat bubbles forming on my nose.

A few people walked out carrying canvas bags and fancy folders. Two of them were Annabelle and George, the young couple who went on dates at La Cocina.

A *beep-beep* made Carmen and me jump out of the way. It was Bicycle Bill, in his tricked-out three-wheeler bike with a basket that carried a huge speaker and his toy poodle, Henry, and had a large picture of Celia Cruz taped to the front. Nobody really knew where Bicycle Bill lived or even where he'd come from, but he had been a fixture of Canal Grove for as long as I could remember. He ate dinner at La Cocina at least once a month. He never said more than three words when he ate. "Hola.

Gracias. Okeydokey." Bicycle Bill turned off the speakers, chained his bike, and took Henry inside.

I glanced at Wilfrido's store closely for the first time. The inside was bright white, and through the window you could see a huge mural with two gold *P*s in the middle. There were white leather chairs organized neatly in two corners of the store, and a large table with several laptops for browsing. I realized that Wilfrido's store wasn't a store at all. It was an office.

An office having a party. People picked at a buffet table filled with sweet and savory pastelitos and cups of cafecito. There was a huge replica of a city near the window. It looked a lot like my neighborhood, only it had a huge tower at the corner of what was Main Street.

"No me gusta eso," Bicycle Bill blurted loudly as he walked back outside. "Nah. Nah." I guess he knew more than three words after all.

Carmen whispered something to me, but I couldn't hear her over my loud, heavy breathing. She whispered again as we went inside, but I still couldn't hear her. Air-conditioning blasted through the holes in my mask, instantly cooling my costume and drying my sweat. I paused for a few seconds to take in the gloriousness.

"Arturo? Arturo?"

"Huh? Oh, sorry," I said. "I was dying out there."

"Try walking five blocks in heels in this heat," Carmen said.

It seemed like everyone from Canal Grove had received an invitation to Wilfrido Pipo's fancy office party. My seventh-grade language arts teacher, Ms. Patterson, and the school librarian, Ms. Minerva, chatted excitedly by the model of the town. There was another long table across the back wall that had a few fancy glass pitchers with mint leaf stems that jutted out of the tops. This kid from my school named Eddy Strap and his parents delicately ate some of the mini-quiches that were plated perfectly next to the mint juice. Eddy and I didn't hang out; he was pretty full of himself.

"I simply love that this building will bring a new kind of person to the neighborhood," Eddy's mom said in a way that sounded snooty.

Wait, what building?

"Come, Juancito, look at the pretty building!" I guess Carmen wanted to find out about this building too.

"Who's Juancito?"

"You are," Carmen whispered. "Juancito, my younger brother."

"That's so weird."

"Just go with it." Carmen put her arm around my shoulders and spoke to me like I was five years old.

"Isn't it interesting?" she said again, making a point to show me the tall building in the center.

The mini high-rise had the same initials as this office— PP—in gold cursive on the front.

I took a closer look but was distracted by the sound of clinking glass as people gathered around the model.

Wilfrido Pipo emerged wearing the same white suit and hat I'd seen him in at La Cocina, smiling brightly at everyone he passed. He politely made his way to the model and stopped right next to Carmen. His eyes narrowed and I could feel beads of sweat forming on my nose once again. Wilfrido would bust us for sure.

"Hello," he said as he patted my shoulder.

"Uh, uh, uh," I mumbled, and looked away at the model.

Carmen held her hand out and pulled me close.

"He likes your display."

"Excellent. I'm very glad," Wilfrido said.

He turned to Carmen and smiled. "What a nice kid. Now, if you'll excuse me, I must address the room."

He tapped his glass again and started. "Everyone! I am new to town and can say that the people of this neighborhood are truly wonderful."

To make his point, Wilfrido put his arm around me and almost knocked off my mask.

"Uh, uh, uh," I mumbled again, shifting around and trying to keep my face hidden. Even if Wilfrido didn't recognize me, every neighbor in this room would.

"Oh, I'm sorry," he said. "Here—let me help you adjust that."

"No!" Carmen yelled, and stood between us. "Ahem,

I'm sorry. He, he just doesn't like anyone touching his mask. Isn't that right, Juancito?"

I nodded and Wilfrido took his arm off me. "I'm so sorry. My sincerest apologies."

It happened very quickly, but I could've sworn Wilfrido rolled his eyes as he apologized.

"As I was saying, this is a beautiful town, full of beautiful, hardworking people."

I looked around and took in the crowd. He was right.

"So it is with this," Wilfrido continued, "that I hope to make a contribution to the neighborhood. Presenting: a new facility to reward your hard work and make your community even stronger."

Wilfrido pointed to the high-rise in the display. "In the next few weeks, I will be speaking with all of you and showing you how this building, Pipo Place, will be the cornerstone and future of this community!"

Carmen and I were pushed to the side as the crowd moved in closer to the model.

"This multi-use building is a state-of-the-art property designed to fit your every need. It will include a high-end grocery store, personalized parking for residents who live on the upper floors, a ten-thousand-square-foot gym, spa, an Olympic-size pool, and a therapy center with free spin classes and daily yoga."

"For everyone who lives in Canal Grove?" Eddy's mom asked excitedly.

"No, unfortunately. But anyone in the neighborhood can apply to become members and have access to many of the facilities."

"Many or all?"

"Many," Wilfrido said, still smiling brightly. "May I continue?"

Wilfrido pointed to each section of the building and continued to describe one incredible thing after another. "There will be a rooftop lounge so patrons can enjoy views of the water. Cafés on five floors so residents and members don't have to go down to the street to get their morning cafecitos, like I know you all love!"

The crowd nodded in agreement. They seemed to marvel at what Pipo Place would contain.

"So," he said, suddenly serious, "this is a place I'm confident the neighborhood and community will love. And hopefully, it's just the beginning! Think of the possibilities: this building will attract more people to the neighborhood. It will create jobs, bring money into the community, and add a level of luxury that the town deserves! Pipo Place will be the crown jewel of Canal Grove!"

Carmen looked like she had just eaten a really disgusting cookie and couldn't understand why everyone else thought it was delicious.

"Well," Wilfrido said, putting his hands together in a prayer pose. "A very important vote is happening in a few weeks—one that will change the face of Canal

Grove and provide a new and exciting opportunity for the wonderful citizens of this community. Can I count on your support? Will you let your city council know how much you want Pipo Place?"

I watched as people applauded. Our city commissioner, Tomás García, patted Wilfrido's shoulder. Eddy's mom looked at Eddy and nodded. My teachers smiled as if they had just heard the most wonderful news.

"¡Perfecto! Now please, enjoy the food and cafecito! And don't leave without these leather tote bags specially made from the finest cows in all of Argentina!"

Carmen and I watched as Wilfrido mixed and mingled. I glanced at the mini-version of Main Street and had to admit—Pipo Place looked nice. A huge building in the neighborhood couldn't be all that bad, could it? The model had a tiny version of Two Scoops. All the people living at Pipo Place would surely go buy ice cream. I saw the little Spanish columns and gated entrance of Books and More Books. Everyone's favorite bookstore would get more visitors. The boutique clothing stores, several neighborhood art galleries, and other local restaurants and cafés were all part of the model. Pipo Place would bring people closer to Main Street—more hungry customers for La Cocina de la Isla. Except . . . La Cocina didn't seem to be part of this model.

I looked at Carmen through my rubber mask and tugged at her dress to get her attention.

"Where's La Cocina in the display?" I whispered.

Carmen's eyes widened.

In this version of town, Pipo Place took over the entire corner of Main Street. La Cocina de la Isla was nowhere to be found. My skin felt hot, my stomach dropped, and I had trouble breathing again. Not even the AC could calm me down. I turned to walk out of Wilfrido's office when I felt a tug at my shoulder.

"Wait, little boy," Wilfrido said. "Take this as a token of my thanks."

He handed Carmen and me each a fancy leather tote. Wilfrido smiled, but it didn't feel friendly this time. I don't know why, but I was pretty sure he'd known who we were all along. "Enjoy," he said.

Once we were out of his line of sight, Carmen took off her heels and I pulled off my mask and Hulk bodysuit. We walked in silence. My tank top was completely drenched in sweat. As we got closer to home, I realized we had both put our things into Wilfrido's fancy bags. The bags were very useful, and suddenly I felt more uncomfortable than I did wearing the mask. We got home, and Uncle Frank asked Carmen to help prep dinner. She said we should meet up after to figure out what to do.

A few hours later I found Carmen in the courtyard, really fired up.

8

chocolate doesn't make things better

"YOU KNOW, I was thinking hard about this, and I can't believe Wilfrido didn't include La Cocina de la Isla. ¡Qué presumido! He doesn't have the authority to do that!" Carmen didn't normally speak Spanish to me. That was how I could tell she was really upset.

We walked around Canal Grove, and my brain fired off more thoughts than I could handle. Pipo Place was huge. It was clear that Wilfrido wanted it to take up more space on Main Street. The only place to expand was *into* La Cocina. Wilfrido couldn't kick us out, but what if my family couldn't renew our lease for some reason? What if Wilfrido knew our lease was up soon and was willing to wait it out?

"We need to tell your mom, right?" Carmen snapped me out of this very depressing game of What If.

"I dunno," I said. When we got to the light at the crossing, I turned to Carmen. "I think we should tell Abuela."

"I don't think that's a good idea, Arturo. It might upset her too much."

"It's Abuela's restaurant. She has more right to know than anybody."

"I just don't think it's a good idea to tell her, Arturo. She was coughing pretty bad the other day."

It was a little after eight o'clock. The sky was beginning to turn into a mix of orange, pink, and gray, with clouds interrupting in patches all over the horizon. I needed time to clear my head, so we took the long way home and stopped at one of my favorite canals. It had a massive tree next to it, with long vines that you could use to plunge into the water.

"This place is really cool," Carmen said as we sat at the edge of the little hill overlooking the canal. The vines from the banyan tree hung over us like they were waiting to turn us into puppets.

"Can you really swing on those?" she asked.

"You have to know the right moment to let go or you'll flop backward into the water and hurt yourself."

"Is it safe in there?" she asked. "Do any animals live in the water?"

The canals that ran through town twisted and turned and eventually dumped out into the bay. That was how the neighborhood had gotten its name.

"Yeah, manatees. If you have a water hose, they come right up and drink from it. They have whiskers and a nose like an elephant whose trunk didn't fully grow."

"And they're not dangerous?"

"Nah, they're kind of goofy-looking, actually. I don't get why people love them so much."

"Maybe because they know they're not dangerous. It's nice knowing an animal that big isn't going to hurt you."

"I guess so," I said. "It's usually the smaller animals that are dangerous around here. Like barracudas. Those things are nasty."

"I've heard of those! They have huge teeth and really slick bodies and nasty, beady eyes."

"Have you seen one?"

"On an animal show once."

We sat in silence a bit while watching the water reflect the pink and orange sky on its surface. I threw in little clumps of dirt that broke up as soon as they met the water. They burst into little clouds that slowly sank to the bottom of the canal, and I wondered how many creatures would come out once night had fallen.

"I'm sorry about everything," Carmen said.

I didn't look up from the water.

"You really want to tell Abuela?" she asked.

"Yeah," I said, digging my hands into the grass and tugging at the blades to pull them free.

"I miss my mom so much," she offered suddenly, and I looked up to see her staring off into space. "I'm tired of being positive about it all the time. It actually really stinks, you know?"

I nodded.

"My mom was amazing," Carmen continued. "She was one of the most respected food writers anywhere."

"Her articles are what got La Cocina de la Isla recognized internationally," I said, because I had read Carmen's mom's food blog. She had been really funny but never snarky when judging food or restaurants.

Carmen's lip twitched like it was charged with electricity. Her face turned red and she let out a breath that sounded like a horse exhaling.

"My dad tells me to think of the good moments," she said, managing a smile.

"What was it like, living in Madrid?" I asked.

"Fine, I guess," she said. "We used to travel so much, you know? Then my mom suddenly started feeling bad and then we stopped traveling."

"When did she, you know, get sick?"

"It happened so fast. She was fine just last year; then it spread so quickly, there was nothing that could be done."

"Food and writing are how our moms met," I said, trying to change the subject.

Carmen smiled. "They were both young and creative and more interested in focusing on the good things that food can be rather than all the criticisms."

"My mom can be pretty critical," I said, and Carmen laughed.

"Yeah, I guess that's true."

Carmen took out a pack of gum and offered a piece to me.

"No, thanks," I said, and looked up to see night quickly closing in. "We should get going," I added. "It's going to get dark soon."

Carmen pulled herself up. The only thing that broke our silence on the walk home was Carmen chewing gum. It wasn't obnoxiously loud or anything. It's just that the neighborhood was really quiet. I thought about how that could change with so many people moving into Pipo Place.

We walked through the gates of our complex, and I stopped just in front of Abuela's apartment. When Abuela had moved in, my mom and dad had wanted to give her a quieter unit away from the gate so she wouldn't have to hear everyone coming in and out. But Abuela refused. She *wanted* to see everyone. Practically every family member stopped into Abuela's on their way home from work or school or wherever.

On the way to Carmen's, we passed the floribunda bush that hadn't sprouted a bud. Carmen dug into her pockets for keys.

"Here they are," she said, then unlocked the door. She opened and called for her dad, but he wasn't there. Carmen shrugged, turned on the lights, and walked to the kitchen.

"Want to come in for a sec for some chocolate?" she asked, opening the cupboard and pulling out a huge bar wrapped in foil.

"Um, sure. Thanks," I said, wondering if it was okay that her dad wasn't home.

"Seventy-two percent cocoa and raspberry. That's my weakness," she said.

I took the piece she offered and practically swallowed the whole thing.

"Whoa! Monster bite! If I did that, I'd get chocolate stuck in every one of my braces."

"Oh, sorry. I guess I was hungry or something."

"Don't be sorry. I could probably eat chocolate all day long if my dad let me."

The living room smelled like mint and licorice, and I wasn't sure where it was coming from. Maybe it was one of those strange wooden boxes hanging from the corner of her ceiling? They had little holes in them and looked like someone had put dried leaves inside.

They had put a few pictures up too, and there was a stack of CDs on top of the credenza.

"My dad loves jazz CDs," she said, shuffling through the collection.

"Why doesn't he just download music?" I asked.

"I don't know. I guess he likes actually putting the CD in a player and waiting for it to cue up to a song. He put all these into a box and checked it on the plane along with all our pictures and a few things from home."

Carmen picked up a frame next to her dad's CD collection and stared. She turned and showed me a photo of her and her parents by the ocean.

"That's the same beach we went to when we visited you guys."

"Yeah," she said, putting the photograph back down and giving me a sad sideways look. "I totally understand why you want to tell Abuela."

I rubbed the edges of a little vase that sat on the counter.

"But you know," Carmen said, "she hasn't been feeling that well, from what my dad tells me."

"That doesn't mean she can't still know things," I said, feeling frustrated.

It suddenly became really hard to be in the same room with Carmen.

"Look, I should get going," I said, starting for the door. "I don't want your dad to come in when we're here by ourselves."

"You're right," she said.

I walked out carrying the fancy leather tote from Wilfrido's office. Then I took out my mask and Hulk bodysuit and tossed the tote into the trash bin. I made my way to Abuela's apartment to talk to her. Through the window, I could see she had fallen asleep on her recliner while watching her favorite telenovela, *El comandante y la duquesa*.

That show was crazy. It was about a wealthy English duchess whose spoiled kids pretended they loved her but were really just trying to cheat her out of her money. But then the duchess married el comandante, a former general in the Chilean army who wore his uniform every day. One of the duchess's kids killed him, but then his twin brother, a commander in the Uruguayan air force who nobody knew existed, showed up and fell in love with the duchess. Now the kids were plotting to kill him, too. That was all I knew, because it wasn't like I watched *La duquesa* regularly.

Anyway, Abuela looked so peaceful, and I hated the idea of causing her stress. As much as I didn't want to admit it, maybe Carmen was right.

What I really needed was to talk to my best friends. Tomorrow was their last day in town before Mop went to camp and Bren left on his family vacation to the Dominican Republic. They'd know what I should do. I ran straight to my room and climbed into bed early so this terrible day would end.

9

keep calm and dale: a dialogue

THE NEXT DAY, Bren invites us over to jump in his bounce house. There is a slide attached to it that leads to Bren's pool. When it gets too hot we like to slide into the water to cool down. Mop is already there, bouncing with Bren.

ME: Guys, something awful happened yesterday.

BREN: Did you lose an arm?

ME: What? No, Bren, my arm is clearly still attached to my body.

BREN: Right. Good thing, dude.

ME: You know that guy who threw in a bid for the lot by the restaurant?

MOP: Wilfrido Pipo?

ME: Yeah. He's got this mega-building he's planning to construct right on Main Street.

MOP: My dad told me about that. I can't believe it's going to have a movie theater inside.

BREN: *What? A movie theater!* Dude, that's the awesomest thing I've ever heard.

ME: I mean, yeah, that is pretty cool, but there's something really bad about it. La Cocina de la Isla isn't in his building plans. If he wins, I think he's going to fight to have La Cocina torn down.

Bren jumps back like he has just heard a gunshot.

BREN: Who does that perfectly dressed man think he is?!

MOP: Why are you yelling?

BREN: Are you not listening? La Cocina de la Isla is under attack. By an amazingly smooth dude who wants to build a sick state-of-the-art building!

MOP: That would be terrible, man.

ME: I know! People work at La Cocina, people who aren't just in my family. We can't leave them without jobs.

BREN: Hold up, bro. They're cooks and waiters. They can find jobs anywhere.

I feel blood rush to my cheeks and a sudden urge to tackle Bren. Mop notices and steps between us.

MOP: Bren, this is bad news, okay? You should be more sensitive.

BREN: I know. I'm just, I dunno.

MOP *(inspecting Bren's face)*: Are you crying?

BREN: What? No. Shut up!

Bren acts like an idiot when something scares him. His favorite restaurant in the world is La Cocina de la Isla. Where most kids want themed birthday parties at chain restaurants, Bren always wants Abuela's legendary arroz con pollo and La Cocina's famous homemade mint juice.

BREN: I'm sorry, dude. I . . . I just couldn't stand to see La Cocina go! ¡El restaurante! Mi patria. I mean, we gotta do something!

MOP: Don't start talking like that again, dude.

BREN: Like what?

MOP: Like you're Pitbull.

BREN: Man, don't diss me, homie! I'm from the 305, dale. ¡Representar mi gente!

MOP: You realize you sound like an idiot, right?

ME: Guys! Focus! What should I do?

Bren makes a fist, taps his chest, and extends his arm to fist-bump me.

BREN: We'll get this, hermano.

MOP: Why are you doing that?

BREN: That's how we do in Havana! We fight back!

MOP: You are not from Havana! Your mom is originally from Cape Cod, and your dad had family on the *Mayflower*!

BREN: You shouldn't be hatin' like that, dude. No es cool.

MOP: How did you find out all this info, Arturo?

ME: Wilfrido's office, with Carmen. He gave this whole presentation about how the building would be good for the town. And how this is just the beginning.

MOP: That sounds ominous, dude. Did you tell your mom?

ME: Not yet.

MOP: What did Carmen say?

ME: I, um . . . I . . . She was, um . . .

Mop and Bren look at me suspiciously.

BREN: Dude, did you wear what I told you to on your date?

ME: It wasn't a date! We were spying on Wilfrido!

BREN: Hey, man, whatever you wanna call it. Spy mission with your godsister. Or date with a gorgeous Spanish girl who has an adorable accent.

MOP: Let the man be, Bren. He's confused enough as it is.

I suddenly don't feel like bouncing anymore.

BREN: I expect daily reports on your progress, Arturo.

MOP: I'm leaving you my *Black's Law Dictionary*. There might be some legal info you could use to battle Wilfrido. And remember, my dad works at city hall. If you need any help from him, just ask.

ME: Thanks, dude.

Bren bounces and talks at the same time.

BREN: The more details, the better! Especially if you two make out.

ME: What?

BREN: Carmen, dude! You guys have been spending some serious QT together.

Bren pretends he is dancing with someone, then twirls around and tries to dip himself. Instead he falls back and rolls into a corner of the bounce house and gets stuck. We hop over to lift him up, and when we finally drag him to his feet, he jumps right back into his story.

BREN: Hey, just tell her, "Carmen, mi amor. I love you, baby!"

Mop and I stare while Bren wraps his arms around himself and twists his neck, pretending to kiss someone.

MOP: You look like a zombie trying to eat its own neck.

Bren stops and turns around.

BREN: Arturo, obviously Carmen is interested in you—hanging out with you all over the place. Chillin' with Abuela. The girl. Is totally. Into you.

ME: You're crazy, dude. No way she likes me. And anyway, if she did, I'm not interested in her like that.

Mop and Bren stop bouncing and give each other a look.

ME: What? I don't like Carmen! Guys, it's just . . .

the people in the neighborhood looked like they really supported Wilfrido's proposal, you know? And what's going to happen to the restaurant if Wilfrido builds that massive high-rise?

BREN: Remember what Pitbull says: "Keep calm and dale."

MOP: I can't believe a Pitbull quote is actually making sense.

BREN: It does? I mean, yeah, of course it does! What was my point?

MOP: That you have to keep going no matter what. You have to fight like you believe you can win.

BREN: Like you and Carmen.

ME: Could you stop talking about Carmen?

BREN: You got it. We're here for you, hermano.

Mop rolls his eyes. Bren either doesn't notice or pretends not to notice. He pulls out his cell phone to check himself out on his camera.

BREN: Guys, I think I'll have a full beard by the time we're in eighth grade.

MOP: You're going to have a beard in three months?

BREN: Don't be jealous.

Bren rubs his face quietly and Mop shakes his head.

MOP: I wonder why we're friends sometimes.

I manage a smile. I am going to miss them when they leave.

The next day I go to Bren's house to say good-bye. Mop

is there to hang while his parents get everything ready for the drive north.

Bren comes out of his room, sporting a half-unbuttoned guayabera and a rhinestone cross dangling from a sparkly silver chain. It looks like it is from his mom's jewelry box. Mop's parents eventually pick him up, and they drive off to Withlacoochee River Wildlife Exploration Summer Camp, somewhere in central Florida. Bren's ride to the airport shows up, and as I say good-bye, I get that sinking, empty feeling when someone leaves but you stay behind.

10

hidden recipes

I LEFT BREN'S house and headed to La Cocina to find my mom. Mop's first instinct had been to tell my mom about Wilfrido's plans, so maybe Carmen was right. I got to the restaurant, and Mari said my mom had gone home for the day. Maybe my mom already knew. It's not like Wilfrido Pipo was hiding it. The model was on display in his window. Anybody could see it!

I walked into my apartment to find my mom putting away some groceries in the kitchen.

"Mom?" I said, trying to get her attention.

Her phone rang, and when she saw the number calling, she picked up.

"Not now, Arturo," she whispered. "Go to your room, please. I need to take this call."

She turned her back to me as she spoke to the person on the phone. "Yes, hello, Andrew. No, nobody is around. What's up?"

It was Mop's dad. I kept listening as I walked away.

"He did? They approved that? Okay, thanks for the heads-up."

My mom let out a long sigh and then turned around, but before she could see me, I was already in my room.

I paced around, trying to figure out what Mop's dad had told my mom. What did they approve? Wilfrido Pipo's plan? I sat at my desk, looking for something to distract me, when I came across Abuelo's box. I had forgotten about it, but there it was, inviting me to open a letter and forget my troubles.

I closed my door and opened the box. Sifting through it, I placed all the contents on my desk: a CD, a whole bunch of letters, a few pens, a watch that didn't work, and a folded envelope that said, in all caps:

PARA ARTURO ZAMORA, MI QUERIDO NIETO. LEÉ ESTO PRIMERO.

Then under the Spanish, a translation:

FOR ARTURO ZAMORA, MY BELOVED GRANDSON. READ THIS FIRST.

Huh? I opened the envelope and pulled out the letter inside. It was handwritten in Spanish, with English translations on the side. My abuelo's print was very neat and didn't waste any space. Every inch of the page was covered. I read a few lines in Spanish, then I glanced over to the English.

My Dear Arturo,

No doubt you will soon speak English much better than I and perhaps without the slightest hint of an accent! Did you know that right now you are four years old and you speak Spanish perfectly?

Totally weird. Maybe that was why I sometimes used Spanish words when English words couldn't fully explain what I needed to say. Like, the puro desastre that was going on with La Cocina. I could take Spanish one or two words at a time, but it was harder to put full sentences together. And forget about asking me to read it. Reading in Spanish was like putting on Abuela's thick glasses and trying to pour cereal into a bowl. I did that once and got so dizzy, I almost fell face-first into my Cocoa Yums.

So perhaps you are reading this as a young man and wondering what on earth

your abuelo is doing, leaving you a box
full of letters and music and poetry.

Yep, that was pretty much true, Abuelo.

Perhaps you are thinking, your abuelo
was a bit loquito, leaving you so much
paper to sift through and ponder. Well,
rather than hearing stories about me
from your parents, or even your abuela,
I wanted to let you discover for yourself
who your abuelo was. So this box contains
every detail of my journey—every
challenge, failure, triumph, and success.
Let us begin with the first thing. Find the
letter in the box marked: El amor y la fe.

Love and faith? That was the phrase Abuela had
said the other day. Why did Abuelo want me to start
there? I unfastened the bundle of letters, carefully
looking for it.

EL AMOR Y LA FE—
LOVE AND FAITH

I unfolded the letter. It was also written in English
and Spanish! How long did it take him to write all these?

The great Cuban poet and patriot José Martí wrote and translated many works of poetry and essays in both English and Spanish. Did you know that a poem by José Martí inspired a very famous song called "Guantanamera"? And that a young man composed a version of it that became a worldwide hit? It is the most famous song in all of Cuba. Probably one of the most famous songs in the world! So you see? A young person has the power to do many great things. It's about belief. And most important, it is about

"Love," I said out loud. I didn't even have to look at the page to know what he was going to write.

love. Love is two spirits meeting, joining together, holding each other, helping raise each other from the earth. It is born in the journey of looking for each other, fed by the need to be together. It is incapable of ever breaking apart! Love is not a tempestuous sea; it is a calm river. It is not a bonfire but a quiet ember. It is not an abrupt end; it is peace.

Huh?

That is what José Martí wrote about love. Don't worry if you don't understand it now. Keep it in your box and go back to those words from time to time. They will begin to make sense as you continue to read and reread them. It took me years to understand the full depth of Martí's words. But eventually this is what I learned.

I learned that no matter what I physically lost on that journey between countries, my history never changed. Because your abuela was with me. As were your mother, aunt, and uncle. I had you and your cousins close to my heart. I had my sister, Tía Abuela Josephina, and her children with me. We had first cousins and second cousins and even third cousins with us! One by one, our family came together in this new land.

We fight, we Zamoras! We fight for what we believe in. We fight for family. We fight to preserve our sense of home. We fight to be just and fair and above all, we fight for love. No form of exile or malady can defeat us. It is invincible.

The rest of these letters have dates on them. They tell my history in order. Read them and learn from the past. And remember to be adventurous, my Arturo. Be alive! Be in love. Find your voice. Find your story. And remember: sometimes life's answers are hidden in poetry.

Tu abuelo,
Arturo Miguel Zamora

I couldn't resist opening another letter. The one marked *1972* told the story of Abuelo in Cuba, working as a taxi driver. He drove around the famous Malecón, a huge seawall along a district in Havana called Vedado, taking tourists from Europe and Canada to Havana's major sights: the museum, the palace, through the cobblestoned streets leading to the University of Havana, and around to the famous nightclubs, like the Tropicana. He wrote that no matter how hot the sun got, the sound of the ocean spraying against the walls of El Malecón was enough to keep you cool. Then one day, he wrote, he noticed a young woman carrying several bags of laundry on a quiet street just around the corner from El Malecón. He stopped the cab and asked if she needed a ride. At first the young woman didn't want to accept the ride, so Abuelo parked his taxi and offered to carry the laundry wherever she needed to go.

But she said she didn't need help. She kept telling me to go away! Soon I retreated to my taxi and drove next to her as she walked. She stopped, turned to me, and said if I didn't leave her alone, she was going to chase me with a machete! She was the toughest, most beautiful woman I had ever met. I apologized and left her alone. On one fateful occasion, while I drove through the same neighborhood, a vicious rainstorm swept through the streets, and your abuela got caught in the middle of it. Sometimes storms come out of nowhere in Cuba. Such is life on the island! I saw her huddled under the awning of a building that was closed. The rain whipped sideways with every gust of wind. She was getting soaked! And so were her freshly laundered clothes. I stopped the car and got out. I told her she could stay in my taxi with her laundry and I would wait outside until the rain stopped. She finally accepted. I gave her the keys to my taxi and she waited inside while the storm subsided. This is how I first met and fell in love with your abuela.

Without thinking, I put the letter down and looked at my computer screen. I logged on to Twitter and typed *Carmen Sánchez* into the search box. A picture of a heart drawn in the sand came up next to the handle @CARSAN2121. I checked and saw that @CARSAN2121 was from Madrid and loved the beach, crime fiction, and poetry. It had to be Carmen, so I sent a direct message.

> @ARTZAM3: hey, is that you, carmen? it's me, arturo.

Every second that she didn't respond felt like an hour. Still nothing. It was a dumb idea to send her a DM. What if it wasn't her? I went to close the screen when a message popped up.

> @CARSAN2121: hi, arturo!

I felt instantly relieved it wasn't some weird stranger.

> @ARTZAM3: hey, so what's up?

> @CARSAN2121: hey, nothing. look, sorry about earlier.

> @ARTZAM3: it's fine.

@CARSAN2121: hey, so i did some digging about wilfrido pipo. i think i found something.

@ARTZAM3: ?

@CARSAN2121: want to meet after your shift at the restaurant?

@ARTZAM3: k

@CARSAN2121: k, my dad is home now. i have to go. bye. c ya. ☺ xoxo.

Carmen signed off, but I continued to stare at my computer screen. Those *x*'s and *o*'s didn't mean anything. Did they? I looked at Abuelo's box and thought about the first time he'd met Abuela. He had not given up. That was what I was going to do: show Carmen that I wouldn't give up. I was going to save the restaurant!

11

adding mucho más

AFTER MY DISHWASHING shift the next day, I waited patiently for Carmen in the dining room at La Cocina. I sat at one of the empty tables in the back and watched as guests finished their lunches and went about their days. From where I was sitting I could hear a few different conversations. They were all talking about the exciting new building.

"Can you believe the gym they're going to have?" said Ms. Prado, a lady who wore too much makeup and always seemed to be wearing workout clothes.

"It's going to be aaammmaaazing!" her friend said.

I always thought those ladies were really funny, and I liked that they came to the restaurant to eat after exercising. But now I found myself getting annoyed at how loud they spoke. Two guys who I knew worked at the bank on the corner leaned over their table to join the conversation.

"Oye, pero did you see that there's going to be a pool on the roof *and* one on the second floor? How sick is that?"

"Man, I'm totally buying an apartment there."

"For sure! It's a dope investment opportunity."

I was totally shocked when I overheard Annabelle and George talking.

"Maybe instead of buying a house, we look into a place in the new building?"

"What?!" I accidently blurted out.

Annabelle and George turned around, but I put a menu up so they wouldn't see me.

I couldn't believe people were eating at La Cocina, enjoying our food, and talking about how cool Pipo Place was going to be. Didn't they realize that if there were a Pipo Place, there would be no La Cocina? Maybe they didn't notice La Cocina was missing from Pipo's plans.

The door opened and Carmen walked in with Abuela, which I didn't expect. The chatter stopped. It was like all forty plus people in the restaurant quit talking at the same time. That didn't stop Abuela from being Abuela. She took Carmen by the hand and greeted several tables by introducing Carmen. Abuela stroked Carmen's hair as she explained who she was, and Carmen politely accepted the compliments the guests gave her. I felt a little rush of heat in my cheeks when I saw Carmen smiling, but it was probably because I was still hot from being in the kitchen for five hours.

Aunt Tuti followed Abuela nervously, like a chicken pecking around for seeds. She kept telling her, "Mami, siéntese," but Abuela didn't want to sit down. Greeting guests was what Abuela loved most besides cooking and family. Carmen scanned the restaurant and saw me sitting at the corner table. As she walked toward me, she smiled, and her shiny, colorful braces lit up the room. Her smile was almost too bright, so I looked down at the tabletop and started inspecting the silverware for any spots or stains.

"So," she said. "Good shift?"

"It was fine," I said. "I wish Martín didn't wear Mira Bro. It's nasty, smelling that deodorant mixed with food and dirty plates for five hours."

"I can imagine. So, like I said, I did a little more digging, and look what I found."

Carmen pulled up something on her phone and handed it to me. It was an article from a local paper in northern Florida, talking about a word I had never heard before: *gentrification*.

"What does that word mean?" I asked Carmen.

"It's when wealthy people come into a neighborhood

to redevelop it to increase its value. It usually pushes out people and businesses that have been around for a long time."

"Do you think that's what Wilfrido is doing?"

"It's what he's been doing in different towns," she said. "Scroll down—see here?"

Apparently, Wilfrido Pipo had built other luxury high-rises in coastal towns around the country. They all looked exactly the same as the one he'd proposed in Canal Grove.

"Whoa, he's got, like, ten other buildings."

"Yeah, and that's not the worst part. Here, check this out," she said, pointing.

I looked at a page:

REQUEST FOR PROPOSALS FOR THE PURCHASE & DEVELOPMENT OF PROPERTY OWNED BY THE CITY

It was the same kind of proposal my mom had put in for the expansion. But this was a new one. It was a request for the purchase of the land right next to the parking lot. The land that La Cocina was on. I kept reading, and my mouth went completely dry. Wilfrido Pipo's name was on the proposal to lease the property.

"How can he do this?!" Carmen yelled so loud, she startled Mr. Michaels, the guy who owned Books and

More Books. He nearly spilled his ceviche all over himself.

"Perdón," Carmen said, offering him a napkin.

"That must be what my mom was talking about on the phone with Mop's dad."

"But it needs to be approved. The city needs to say yes."

"Yeah," I said, and realized I hadn't seen Commissioner García at La Cocina for lunch with his staff. "I don't know; something doesn't feel right."

Abuela slowly shuffled to our table, carrying two large glasses filled to the rim with creamy orange smoothies. "Dos batidos de mango," she said as she handed us the glasses garnished with little mango wedges.

"Gracias, Abuela," I said. I shifted uncomfortably, like I was literally sitting on top of all of the secrets I was keeping from Abuela. She smiled and motioned for me to drink my batido, but I just couldn't do it. I couldn't hold everything in anymore. What happened next, I'm not proud of. It was like popping the lid on a pressure cooker before the whistle signaled it was time to open it. Carmen chimed in excitedly in Spanish every time I stopped to take a breath.

Abuela was silent for a long time. She stroked her silk scarf, and every once in a while she looked like she was going to speak and finally put me out of my misery. Carmen stared at Abuela like a pastry chef carefully sprinkling coconut shavings onto white-chocolate cream cheese frosting. Careful. Concentrated. Determined.

Abuela's lips curled into a smirk and finally broke the silence.

"Son un buen equipo," she said, pointing from me to Carmen. Something about Abuela saying Carmen and I made a good team made me think about Abuelo's letter. When did they start thinking of themselves as a good team? I shook my head and tried to focus.

"Abuela, what do we do?" I asked.

"Habla con tu mamá, Arturo."

I tried to tell Abuela that talking to my mom was pointless. Mom was too busy, and she'd probably just tell us to keep "business as usual."

"Abuela, we could lose the restaurant!"

She looked serious for a moment and glanced at Carmen again.

"¿Te dije cómo tu abuelo y yo nos conocimos, Arturo?"

"Yes, Abuela," I told her, wondering why in the world she was talking about meeting Abuelo for the first time.

"Pero," she said. "¿Sabes qué pasó después?"

I didn't know what happened after they'd first met, because I hadn't read any other letters. Carmen pressed her to tell the story, and I started getting impatient with Abuela. Now was not the time to tell family stories! But I knew better than to interrupt Abuela, so I kept my mouth shut while my tapping my fingers on the bottom of the table.

Abuela said that after she agreed to a first date with Abuelo, they became inseparable. Abuelo would pick her up at the laundromat, and together they folded clothes for her entire family. Afterward they would hop into Abuelo's taxi and drive all the way to Abuela's house, where her mother, grandmother, aunts, uncles, and cousins all lived.

"Y después," she said, "cocinaba una cena para él."

She cooked a meal for Abuelo every time he dropped her off at home. Abuela's home, it turned out, was kind of unusual. Her family ran a paladar, which was a restaurant inside someone's house. People from all over the city and plenty of foreigners came to visit her family's paladar. Abuela was one of the best cooks around. And she was only twenty years old!

Abuela laughed. "Pero tu abuelo no era buen cocinero."

Abuelo wasn't so great of a cook, apparently. I remembered how she said he'd burned the steak once. He helped the paladar by serving customers, cleaning dishes, and greeting people while the rest of Abuela's family chipped in where they could. It sounded a lot like how things were run at La Cocina now.

"Nos divertimos mucho," she said, remembering how much fun it was.

One year after they first met, Abuelo and Abuela got married. She smiled and took my hand out from under the table.

"Lo más importante," she said, "es el amor y la fe."

But love and faith weren't going to save the restaurant. What we needed was a plan. We needed to get the family together. We needed to get the community involved. Why wasn't Abuela making sense?

"I know, Abuela, but the restaurant. The neighborhood. We have to fight for it."

"Arturo," she said, staring at me with her blue-gray eyes. "Hay mucho más que eso."

She got up and said she wanted to go home because she was feeling a little tired. Before we left, Abuela said good-bye to every guest in the dining room in her style—stroking faces, caressing hair, and squeezing shoulders.

We walked down the hallway to the kitchen, and she stopped in front of the wall of photographs. She pointed to an old one of her and Abuelo, who was wearing an apron and cap, his big ears sticking out. He was shorter than Abuela, but you could tell he felt like the tallest man in the world. He was smiling with pride at Abuela and her tray of arroz con mariscos, standing in the first restaurant they'd ever run together.

Abuela coughed more than usual on our walk home. We slowed our pace, but it didn't seem to help. By the time we arrived, Abuela had serious trouble catching her breath.

"Let's get her inside," I said, and handed Carmen the

keys. She quickly opened the door, and a blast of freezing-cold air from the AC hit our faces.

I walked Abuela to her bed.

"Abuela? Are you okay?"

"Agua, por favor. Un poco de agua," she said between coughs.

Carmen bolted to the kitchen and brought back some water while I dialed my mom.

"Mom," I said while Carmen gently lifted Abuela upright and held the cup to her mouth. "Abuela won't stop coughing. . . . Okay. . . . Okay."

I hung up and slowly rubbed Abuela's back like my mom told me to. Her coughs slowed down, but my heart sped up. *Be okay. Be okay.* It was the only thought in my mind. Abuela closed her eyes, held her breath, and didn't move.

"Abuela? Abuela!" I yelled. Finally she turned to me, looking dazed.

"Estoy bien, mi amor," she said, slowly grasping for the glass of water.

She reclined. I reached for her palm at the same time Carmen did, and we touched. I went to pull away, but Abuela closed Carmen's hand in mine as her breathing started to steady.

12

behind smiles and good service

MY MOM RUSHED into Abuela's room, still wearing her chef's coat. She gave Abuela some medicine, checked her pulse, and pushed us out so Abuela could rest.

We stood in the living room without saying a word. I could tell my mom was really worried.

"Mom?" I said, walking over to her.

"¿Sí?"

For the second time today, I spilled my guts. I told my mom everything. About visiting Wilfrido's office. About La Cocina missing from his building plan. About how excited people seemed about Pipo Place. About finding out that a proposal by Wilfrido to take over the restaurant's lease had been submitted to the city. I told my mom everything. Todo.

"And you shared this information with Abuela?" she asked.

I nodded.

There was a long pause before my mom turned to Carmen.

"Carmen, can you please give me a minute with Arturo?" Her lips pursed and she looked at me with a face that said, "Just wait till Carmen leaves."

Carmen nodded and excused herself. I braced for the worst as my mom paced around Abuela's living room.

"Arturo, you know that Abuela has a disease that affects her lungs," she said.

"Yes."

"She needs to limit her activities and excitement."

"I just thought, you know, because so many people love her, she might be able to convince the neighborhood to vote against Wilfrido."

My mom exhaled deeply. "Arturo, if we go around acting as if we are desperate to win the favor of the community, then we will fail."

"Is that what you were talking about with Mop's dad?"

"What?" My mom stopped pacing and watched me carefully.

"I overheard you talking to Mr. Darzy. Did you know Wilfrido requested to take over our lease once it expires?"

"Arturo, the city owns the property. And the city board members will vote."

"It's not fair!"

"It's democracy, Arturo. This is how the government runs."

"But we have to do something," I said, raising my voice.

"We're doing what we can."

"We're not doing enough!"

I kept quiet for a second, feeling my lips tighten and my eyebrows narrow.

"You're right," she finally offered, touching my face as if to cool the anger I was feeling. "Let's call a family meeting."

I nodded, feeling good. "When?" I asked.

"Now."

Without saying another word, my mom whipped out her phone and started texting furiously. We had a group family chat going at all times—mostly for fun and sometimes to call meetings. Her phone dinged like crazy, and you could practically hear the nervousness coming through.

"Vamos, Arturo. We're meeting everyone in the courtyard."

One by one, my family members made their way out of their apartments and to the center of the courtyard. Yolanda and Mari argued about a book Mari had borrowed from Yolanda but didn't return, and Brian thought it would be a good to bring his speakers to the *family* meeting. No one was in the mood to hear Flo Rida rapping in the background, and we all let him know it. Carmen came out with her dad and waved to me. Vanessa was at a friend's house and sent many texts asking us to hold off until she got there. My mom didn't want to wait, so Vanessa called me on FaceTime and video-conferenced in.

"Hello?" she said as the video caught up with her voice. "Arturo, press it so I can see everyone."

I could see Vanessa on the screen, pulling out a piece of paper.

"I'll take minutes of the meeting," Vanessa said through the phone. "Arturo, can you walk a little closer to everyone? That's perfect. Thanks."

My mom shook her head and began. "I know everyone isn't here." A few cousins were still at the restaurant.

"I made a note of who isn't here, Tía," Vanessa said.

"Gracias, mi amor," my mom said, and continued. "I think we'll start, and the rest can read Vanessa's notes later."

"What are we discussing, Cari? The art of keeping things as they are and not fighting?"

"No, Tuti, we're going to do something."

"Finally!"

"You should see how many followers Pipo Place has on Instagram," Yolanda blurted out. "He just launched it today!"

"But you're following him also," Mari pointed out.

"I'm following him because I want to see what he's up to, okay?" Mari and Yolanda went on like that for a bit, and soon others chimed in with opinions.

Uncle Carlos spoke up as he tried to keep my twin cousins Benny and Brad from crawling all over him while he pushed the double stroller carrying his other set of twins, Brittany and Brianna.

"We should have proposed to build a daycare in the lot instead," he said. "Wilfrido won't have one of those. We could watch all the kids in the neighborhood."

"Half the kids in the neighborhood are yours, Carlos." Aunt Tuti could be cold sometimes.

"Do you know the likelihood of having two sets of fraternal twins, Tuti? One in three thousand. One. In three thousand."

"What you should have done is played the lotto after the girls were born."

"I did. Didn't get one number right."

"Well, don't play baby lotto again, okay? We only have so many apartments in this complex."

Uncle Carlos was the youngest of Abuela's kids and a stay-at-home accountant. His wife, my aunt Mirta, was an attorney who worked with the state department and had to travel a lot (which is why she sometimes missed Sunday family dinner). As an accountant, Uncle Carlos did the taxes for the family as well as La Cocina in between naps and diaper changes.

"Cari, we need to go to war with this overly perfumed man," Tuti said, getting back on topic. "War!"

"We're not doing any of that, Tuti."

"Then what *are* we doing?"

"We have to make sure we're the best we can be. Everybody, do your jobs with a little extra attention. We don't want anything to go wrong. The city council will vote on both bids in two and a half weeks."

That seemed to get everybody's attention. Yolanda and Mari said they would step up their service. Brian said the drinks would be extra-sweet. The cooks said the food would have a bit more flavor. We all decided the music that played overhead would throw back to the days when the restaurant first opened nineteen years ago—Beny Moré, Celia Cruz, and Tito Puente. My dad vowed to make a special sign to hang outside the restaurant that would say we were celebrating almost two decades and counting.

"It should look like we're not planning on going anywhere," my mom said.

"Cari, making little signs and stepping up service is cute and all, but this is bigger than that," Aunt Tuti said. "Wilfrido Pipo is trying to take us down. We need to fight and fight big!"

"And what do you propose, Tuti? Should we take out machine guns? Or maybe samurai swords?"

"It's better than hiding behind smiles and extra-good service!"

"We are a family-run business, and the neighborhood loves us. Being extra-attentive will remind people of how special our place is. It's just the right touch."

The rest of the family agreed with this plan—except Aunt Tuti, who wanted to take more extreme measures, like banging cazuelas outside of Wilfrido's office at all hours of the day.

After the meeting, everyone went back to their apartments. My mom and Aunt Tuti headed to Abuela's to check up on her. I said good-bye to Vanessa and hung up. I wasn't sure how I felt. I was glad that my family was thinking about stepping up their game, but I wasn't sure it would be enough.

13

ZEMCON 5

WE SPENT THE next week on high alert. Everyone worked harder to make the best possible impression on guests. I washed dishes over and over, and Martín yelled at me a couple of times because I was taking too long to move the dish racks through El Monstruo. It felt like guests were really responding to our extra level of service. We sent out free goat cheese croquets with fresh fig jam to every person who came in to eat. My mom instructed the servers to say it was a thank-you from Abuela. Brian prepared fresh mint juice and poured it into these amazing ceramic jars that said *Agua* in cursive on them. Every table got a jar of fresh mint juice. It was all hands on deck, and the restaurant was buzzing.

Abuela was the only one missing. My mom, Aunt Tuti, and Uncle Carlos insisted that she stay at home so she could take her medicine and rest. But that meant we all had to try to fill the dining room with Abuela's essence—the thing our customers loved more than her cooking.

We had more specials, extended lunch menus into the night—something that a few of our regulars had asked for in the past. Commissioner García finally came back to the restaurant and was especially pleased when he heard he could eat his favorite Cuban sandwich for dinner also. As the week went on, we felt really good about the upcoming vote.

Then everything exploded on Friday morning.

Aunt Tuti was in a total panic. She paced up and down the restaurant, a newspaper in her hand, ignoring all the guests waiting to be seated for lunch.

"Look at this? Look. At. This!" Aunt Tuti practically crammed the *Tropical Tribune* into my mom's face. My mom's eyes bounced left to right as she read, and after a minute her eyes stopped cold on Aunt Tuti's face. In that moment you could tell she was freaked out. That expression was quickly replaced by what looked like a totally fake calm.

"Tuti, right now, you need to do your job and not get hysterical."

"Hyst—"

"Yes, Tuti, hysterical. Take control and go do your job. We are going to figure this out after lunch. Keep it together. I need my sister to be strong. Okay?"

Tuti nodded quietly. It was the first time in my life that I didn't see Aunt Tuti make a face at my mom when she told her to do something. Aunt Tuti went back to the hostess stand to greet a guest.

"Hi! I'm so sorry for the wait. Come—let me get you the perfect table." Aunt Tuti grabbed two menus and walked a couple I didn't recognize over to a table by the window. They looked at La Cocina like it was the first time they had ever been there. Maybe they had just moved into the neighborhood?

Aunt Tuti returned to the hostess stand and took out her phone, texting a million miles an hour. Her lips were pressed tightly together as she stared at her screen. When the door opened, she looked up, and the huge smile returned to her face as she seated another guest. Aunt Tuti really was trying her best to be strong. But why did my mom need that?

My mom had already disappeared into her office, leaving the newspaper behind at the bar. I thought the coast was clear when I grabbed it, but Martín shot me a dirty look and barked at me to get back to work. I quickly scanned the page. There wasn't an article, just what looked like a half-page ad.

PIPO PLACE CELEBRATES
THE COMMUNITY WITH

¡EL FESTIVAL DE LAS ESTRELLAS!

FREE FOOD, DANCING,
AND GIFTS FOR RESIDENTS

JUST THE FIRST OF MANY COMMUNITY
EVENTS COURTESY OF PIPO PLACE

WILFRIDO PIPO LAND HOLDINGS, LLC

SATURDAY, 11 A.M.–8 P.M.,
ON THE CORNER OF MAIN STREET

¡NOS VEMOS!

"Wilfrido Pipo is throwing a festival to promote Pipo Place," I said, showing Martín. "The city votes in two weeks!"

Martín was quiet for a moment before throwing the paper into the garbage and yelling at me to get back to work.

I fastened my apron angrily. Working with Martín was like trying to corral a stubborn water buffalo. Impossible. He checked his phone and must have seen the million messages Tuti had sent to the group chat about the festival, because his face suddenly scrunched up and he kicked over the garbage can. He said Wilfrido's name and then a really bad word I can't repeat. This was going to be a fun shift.

My head pounded as I hung up my apron. As it turns out, when Martín was truly mad—yeah, everything I'd seen up to that point was him being cheery—he liked to blast death metal in the kitchen. I had a clear shot to the front door and bolted before anyone could stop me to talk. That was when my mom appeared and blocked my path to freedom.

"Come with me," she said, taking off her chef's coat and La Cocina de la Isla baseball cap.

"Where are we going?"

"To Wilfrido Pipo's office. He's having a catered lunch for the local businesses."

"Were we invited?" I asked, following my mom outside.

"No," she said, moving quickly from the back alley to Main Street.

I didn't know what to say, so I just nodded and followed her.

Banners hung from the ceiling at Wilfrido's office, and people swatted playfully at gold and silver balloons tied to their chairs. I scanned the room for the model of the town, but it was replaced with a Photoshopped image on the wall of Pipo Place.

"The model of the town isn't here anymore," I said. "It used to be by the window."

Dulce Dominguez, the lady who owned Two Scoops, munched on a crostini that looked like it had red caviar on it. Mr. Michaels suspiciously eyed a meatball and decided he wouldn't try it. Chuchi Flores, who owned the boutique clothing shop down the block, sipped on sparkling red juice while she spoke excitedly with Estelle Anderson, who owned the antique store next to Chuchi's.

"The festival should bring lots of people this weekend," said Estelle. "I told my staff to be ready."

"It's delightful for the community!" said Chuchi, taking a long sip from her champagne flute.

"And for the local businesses," said Wilfrido Pipo. He emerged from behind a door, wearing a bright-blue suit with a pink shirt and sunglasses.

"Oh, it's La Cocina's mother and son. How nice of you to stop by our little gathering." Wilfrido smiled brightly as he walked toward us.

"We didn't seem to get an invitation," my mom said, fake smiling.

"Funny, it was for all the local businesses in the neighborhood. I'll have my assistant look into it."

"Well, we're here now," my mom said.

"I hope the restaurant is able to run without its star chef!" Wilfrido made it a point to talk loudly so everyone heard him.

"The restaurant runs perfectly well even when I'm not there," my mom said, not taking her eyes off of Wilfrido.

"Excellent," Wilfrido said, handing my mom a champagne flute. "Then let's toast to new beginnings!"

My mom took the flute, and the other business owners watched carefully. She smiled and raised her glass high.

"To the businesses of this community," she said. "Thank you for making Canal Grove what it is."

"Hear, hear!" declared Mr. Michaels. "And to La Cocina for being the foundation!"

Soon the rest of the room followed.

Wilfrido raised his glass and quickly took a gulp of his drink. "Let's have the raffle drawing! We're giving away an all-expenses-paid weekend getaway to the Caribbean for two!"

He moved around the room, holding a bowl full of business cards.

"Actually, why don't I pick two different winners? Then four of you can go!"

Wilfrido didn't wait for anyone to respond. He dug his hand inside and pulled out the first business card.

"Chuchi Flores!"

Chuchi's jaw dropped while Estelle clapped excitedly. Everyone grew anxious and excited as Wilfrido scanned the room. He looked at my mom and handed the bowl to her.

"Do you want to pick the next winner, Chef?" he asked.

Enrique Surmallo, the artist who owned a gallery close to La Cocina, approached my mom.

"Don't worry, Cari," he said. "You are part of this community like we all are."

"Exactly!" Wilfrido said as he extended the bowl. "It's all in good fun."

My mom hesitated.

"Don't do it, Mom," I said. "Remember why we're here. The festival."

"How did you get a festival approved on such short notice?" my mom asked, pushing the bowl away.

"Commissioner García is just the nicest man. He loves golf as much as I do."

My mom gave Wilfrido the most intense look, but he didn't seem fazed. In fact, he smiled brighter. His assistant popped up next to him and took pictures with his phone, furiously typing after every picture.

"Claudio is my assistant extraordinaire," he said. "He is posting pictures of all our events. Here, let's take a selfie!"

Before my mom could react, Wilfrido put his arm around her and took a photo. He handed the phone back to his assistant. "The caption should read: 'Chef Caridad and Wilfrido at the local business luncheon for Pipo Place!' Hashtag: working together."

Claudio typed and posted the picture, then left to take one of Chuchi in front of the banner with the raffle information. My mom looked over to me and motioned for us to leave.

"Come on," she said.

"Well, at least throw your business card in there, Chef!" Wilfrido said.

"No, thank you," she replied. She turned to everyone else and managed a smile. "It was nice seeing you all."

We walked out of the office and toward the restaurant. My mom took out her phone and began texting.

Everyone meet at the restaurant today before we open for dinner. ZEM.

With that, her phone went crazy. Two family meetings in one week—and this one was upgraded to a Zamora Emergency Meeting? The last time we'd had a ZEM, Abuela went to the hospital for her third stay in three months, and it was decided that she wouldn't cook Sunday family dinner anymore. ZEM was not a good sign. I could only imagine Aunt Tuti's hysterics back at La Cocina. I looked at my mom as she scowled. Maybe now we'd break out the machine guns and samurai swords.

14

what would abuelo do?

MY MOM AND I walked into the restaurant and waited for the rest of the family to arrive. We were between the lunch and dinner shifts, so the place was empty except for a few cooks preparing for dinner service. My mom checked her phone a few times and then called my dad.

"Apparently he met with Commissioner García, who approved a festival. . . . I know, Robert. I know. . . . Well, what can I tell you? Just come so we can talk about it."

Brian was the last to arrive. By the time he got there, La Cocina was filled with loud and angry Zamoras.

"I told you he was up to no good!" Aunt Tuti yelled, pacing around. "But you are so trusting, Cari."

"He must have been planning this festival all along. It isn't easy to get paperwork approved to do something in the neighborhood," my uncle Carlos complained.

"He probably kissed García's hand like he did mine. Engreído!" Aunt Tuti waved her hand around so wildly, I thought she was going to knock somebody out.

"How come we didn't think about throwing a party for the town?" Mari asked.

"It's too late now. What do we do?" asked Yolanda.

Vanessa jumped up. "Let's hand out informational literature with all the cons of this development clearly outlined!"

Everyone stopped and turned to her.

"Huh?" Martín asked, scratching his chin.

"We can make flyers and pamphlets," she repeated. "And hand them out to everyone at the festival."

"What is the point of that, Vanessa? Residents don't get to vote—only the city council." Martín still looked dumbfounded.

"Don't you know anything?" Vanessa said. "Individual people don't get to vote, but they do get to voice their concerns at the public forum *before* the vote."

"Let's make sure they disapprove *loudly*," Aunt Tuti said, cupping her hands over her mouth like a megaphone.

"Wilfrido Pipo won't let us distribute flyers at *his*

festival," Brian said, throwing himself onto one of the lounge chairs in the greeting area.

"As members of this community," Vanessa argued, "we are entitled to distribute promotional materials about our place of business within three hundred feet of our property. And the festival is taking place on the lot outside, so . . ."

"We are allowed to do it!" Aunt Tuti jumped up and squeezed Vanessa. "Ay, my daughter is a genius. Aren't you, mi amorcita bella?"

"Mom," Vanessa said, peeling away from Aunt Tuti. "You're embarrassing me."

"This is your family, Vanessa," Aunt Tuti said, squeezing tighter. "There is no such thing as embarrassment."

The rest of the family nodded at both Aunt Tuti's statement and Vanessa's plan. It was a good idea.

"Okay," my mom said, "we can distribute flyers tomorrow at the festival. We must make the people of Canal Grove understand what's going on. But for now let's get ready for the dinner shift."

Tuti looked at the reservation book and made a face like she'd just witnessed a flan de coco slip off her plate and splatter onto the floor.

"Well, we don't have to rush," she said. "It's Friday and we barely have any reservations. Where is everyone tonight?"

Nobody knew why we had so few reservations. I

thought about Abuela. Would she call some of her loyal guests? Would she worry like everyone else?

"Maybe I should go check on Abuela," I said suddenly, wanting to be with her.

"Good idea," my mom said. "But please, don't—"

"I know, Mom," I said. "I won't talk to her about the restaurant."

"Thank you," she said, and retreated to the kitchen.

I left the restaurant, kind of bummed. Why didn't we have a normal number of reservations tonight? Would we be able to make a difference with a few flyers and signs? Or would Wilfrido's festival drown out our voices?

I found Abuela rocking quietly in her recliner. Her face broke out into a smile when she saw me.

"Arturito," she said, waving me over.

She had a book on her lap. I must have caught her in the middle of reading.

"Poesía," she said.

Not poetry again. I wish I could have told her about Wilfrido's festival. And about the plans we had to hand out flyers and protest. But I didn't. Abuela exhaled slowly and deeply, wrinkling her face like she knew my mind was full of crazy thoughts. Abuela knew everything.

"Leé un poco, Arturito," she said, handing me the book. The name on the worn-out cover was familiar—José Martí, the poet Carmen liked and the man Abuelo kept talking about in his letters. Were we related to this guy or something? Why was everyone so obsessed with his work? At that, I remembered I hadn't returned Carmen's copy yet. It was still on my desk. I made another mental note to give it back to her soon.

The book made a crackling sound when I opened it. The verses were in Spanish, and I had a feeling I was going to end this reading session with a headache. But if it made Abuela happy, it was worth it. The poem began:

Yo soy un hombre sincero
De donde crece la palma,
Y antes de morirme quiero
Echar mis versos del alma.

The lines had something to do with being sincere . . . and growing in a palm tree? And dying. And wanting to sing a verse from the *alma*, which I thought meant "soul." I read over the next part:

Yo vengo de todas partes,
Y hacia todas partes voy:

Arte soy entre las artes,

En los montes, monte soy.

I had absolutely no idea what that part meant. I flipped to the cover again to give myself a little break.

Versos sencillos was the title. The literal translation was something like "Easy Poems," but trust me, this was *not* easy. Abuela slid her finger between the pages to open the book and then pointed to the first poem again. She tapped the page until I started reading.

Yo soy un hombre sincero

De donde crece la palma,

Y antes de morirme quiero

Echar mis versos del alma.

I read the opening again and tried harder to translate it.

I am a sincere man

From where the palm trees grow,

And before I die, I want

To

. . . um

sing my verses of the soul?

Abuela smiled at me. At least that sounded like actual, understandable English! I even felt a little proud of myself, so I kept reading.

Yo he visto en la noche oscura

Llover sobre mi cabeza

Los rayos de lumbre pura

De la divina belleza.

Okay, this one was much harder. Something about the dark night, but I was pretty sure the poem wasn't about Batman. I felt the pages of Abuela's book between my fingers. Not only did they look and feel like onion skin, they kind of smelled like onion too.

Abuela stared at me. She took the book from my hands and put her palm against the back of my neck. Her eyes hid in the folds of her wrinkled lids. She shuffled to the bookshelf and tucked Martí back into his place.

"Lo mas importante, mi Arturito, es el amor y la fe. Nunca lo olvides."

I reached into my pockets and dug so deep, my fists nearly busted through the lining. Abuela's hands felt cold and leathery against my neck. Even compared to a few days ago, she looked, I don't know, older. Her movements were so stiff. Her gray hair was loose and she wasn't wearing any makeup. Abuela *always* wore makeup. She closed her eyes slowly and then opened them again.

"¿Has leído las cartas de tu abuelo?" she asked.

I hadn't read Abuelo's letters in a few days, I told her. She leaned against the bookcase.

"Estoy un poco cansada," she said, and I helped her to her room. I tucked her into bed and watched as she drifted off to sleep. I wondered how many times in my life Abuela had tucked me in. Probably a million times.

I kissed her cheek and whispered good-bye. I left her apartment, still wishing I could have told her about everything that was going on. But how could I? It wouldn't be fair to get her worked up.

Abuela reminded me that I had a stack of letters from Abuelo waiting to be read. I wondered if Abuelo ever had to hold in a secret this big from someone he loved. I went to my room to be alone with Abuelo's words. I was eager to hear anything he had to say.

1979
EL VALOR—COURAGE

My Dear Arturo,

Sometimes life forces you to make bold decisions. Sometimes those decisions require many sacrifices and choices that will change the course of your journey forever. When Abuela and I left Cuba with our small children, it was no easy thing. We left our homeland, a place we had known all our lives.

I knew this story. Abuelo and Abuela came to the United States from Cuba in 1979. They settled in Miami, where Abuelo found work as a car mechanic and Abuela cleaned houses. That was how Abuela had met a family called the Merritts. She cleaned their home for years. One day the Merritts threw a party. The caterer canceled at the last minute, so Abuela stepped in and cooked dozens of dishes. The party guests were so impressed, the Merritts asked Abuela to cook for all their fancy parties. Word spread of Abuela's talent, and soon she was cooking for private events all over town. Abuelo and Abuela saved money and bought a small lunchtime restaurant in a part of town where most Cuban immigrants went when they arrived here from the island. The restaurant was called La Ventanita. There was a small window that customers could walk up to and get familiar bites like Cuban sandwiches or a bowl of Abuela's chicken soup with chunky potatoes. It was comfort food to a whole group of people who longed for a taste of home. Then nineteen years ago, when Mr. Merritt passed away, he left Abuela some money to open a restaurant in his neighborhood. That restaurant became La Cocina de la Isla.

> *Of course you probably know the history of how we first came to America and how we worked very hard to start our restaurants and build a nice life for our family.*

"Abuela has told me a million times, Abuelo," I said to the letter.

> *And surely you know about the dangerous journey we took across the ocean in order to make a new life in America?*

I wrote a paper about it in class last year.

> *But do you know that this was not the most courageous thing I have ever done?*

Huh?

*No, my dear grandson, that distinction
belongs to the first time I mustered the
courage to tell your abuela I loved
her.*

How was that more courageous than escaping your country in a rickety boat with small children and risking being eaten by sharks or getting caught and sent to prison?

*Your abuela was a very tough woman!
And very beautiful and talented. I was
just a taxi driver who loved to read.
What could I possibly offer such an
incredible lady? What if I told her
I loved her and she rejected me? My
life would be over. I had to find the
right moment. The perfect time to
show her how much I respected and
loved her.*

I felt a rumbling in my stomach, but I wasn't hungry. It was like a deep fryer was sizzling yucca fries in my guts and it felt, um, weird and good at the same time. I knew exactly why my stomach felt this way—it had felt this way ever since a certain girl with colorful braces had walked into La Cocina three weeks ago. I still wasn't sure if it was okay to like Carmen or if she even liked me back, but I had to find out once and for all. My guts depended on it.

I turned back to the letter.

So you know what I did? I imagined what José Martí must have done when faced with such a challenge. I wrote. I wrote a poem for your abuela, telling her how much I loved her. Admittedly, it was the worst poem written in the Spanish language. But still, it gave me the courage to profess my love to her. Letting poetry speak for me was the most unexpected thing I had ever done. I hope one day you will get to do the unexpected, Arturo. It will surprise you beyond anything you will ever experience. Enjoy courage. It is a wonderful thing to overcome fear.

That last line made me feel totally fired up. I folded the letter back into the box, ready to test my courage in more than one way. It was like Abuelo was giving me his mojo through his words. I suddenly felt brave. Bold. Like a fisherman in a rising storm taking the massive waves rolling all around him. I wasn't going to get nauseous. No way. I was going to save the restaurant and, I decided, I was going to tell Carmen how I really felt about her. Abuelo and I shared a name. Maybe we shared courage, too.

15

josé martí doesn't eat churros

ON THE MORNING of the festival, my family gathered in the courtyard. Abuela felt particularly sick, so
my mom decided to stay behind with her.

"You guys will do great. I have faith in you," she said.
"¡Echa pa'lla!"

Vanessa arrived with a whole crew of friends wearing
bright-green T-shirts that said GT. Ali Rodriguez lifted
three boxes of flyers at a time and placed them in neat
piles in a corner. Ali was Vanessa's best friend and the
nicest girl ever. Simon Oliver, the captain of the school
debate team, carefully marked the boxes on a legal pad.
His perfectly combed hair, khaki pants, and loafers with
no socks made him look twenty years older than he really was. Vanessa's other friends, twins Amanda and

Katie, moved swiftly to unfold a table and drape a green cloth over it. Other kids held signs on sticks with different slogans on them.

These kids were the real deal at my school. They organized rallies, had students sign all kinds of petitions—from making drinking water safer to protecting the Key Largo woodrat to planting trees throughout the neighborhood. And their fearless leader? My cousin Vanessa.

"¡Atención, Zamoras!" she said. "This is my environmental group. We call ourselves the Green Teens."

I could see Carmen out of the corner of my eye. She seemed mesmerized by the group, a huge grin spread across her face.

"We stayed up all night, fact-checking and creating the layout for the flyer," Vanessa continued.

"If your school asks why they're out of paper supplies, should I tell them to look for the Green Teens?" Martín said, then laughed.

"Martín, do you want to tell jokes or do you want to save the restaurant?"

Martín actually looked ashamed. It was my turn to laugh.

"And now for some good old-fashioned activism against Wilfrido Pipo," Vanessa said, motioning for her team of student leaders to pass out materials. Next, she used a map to direct family members to their assigned posts at the festival. "The festival takes place primarily in the lot, but it also extends out to here and here." Vanessa made little pink and blue dots where different family members were supposed to stand.

"You got a map of Canal Grove?" I asked.

"You're not the only sneaky Zamora," Vanessa said, winking as she handed me a flyer. "Come on. Let's help people see the light!"

I looked at the flyer, which had Abuela's face right in the middle of it with smaller photos of the rest of my family circled around her. In the background was a watermark of the restaurant, with photos of Abuela posing with different members of the community—including a large photo of Abuela with Commissioner García. The words *We are your family* appeared in cursive on the bottom. I flipped the flyer over to find restaurant stats and a paragraph about the environmental impact of a highrise in Canal Grove.

"How did you get these done so fast?"

"My friend Adrian runs his own graphic design company," Vanessa said, and pointed to a guy unpacking flyers. "His team put it together."

I watched Adrian unpack the flyers from the boxes. His hair jutted out from the sides of his hat, and he had to lift his shorts up every time he bent over to pick up more flyers.

"He's our age?!"

Vanessa nodded. "He can be very immature and he

slacks off a lot, but when it comes to design work, there's nobody better. Great job with the flyers, A."

Adrian looked up and smiled, admiring his work.

Then Carmen walked up, and I felt nervous all of a sudden. I hadn't decided when I was going to tell her yet, but my guess was that during a protest was not a good time.

"Hi, Arturo," she said. She was so close to my face. It was like she was a blowtorch burning my neck and making a crispy marshmallow out of my throat. The fruity body splash she had on made it impossible to focus.

"You okay?" she said, eyeing me like something was wrong with me.

"Huh? Yeah. Sorry."

I thought about Abuelo's letter. Now I knew what he meant about doing the most courageous thing ever. When you decide you're going to tell a girl you like her, you need galactic-level courage.

"Arturo?"

"Right," I said, refocusing. "We'd better get out there before Vanessa gets mad."

My whole family and the Green Teens walked to Main Street together. My cousins who we called cousins but weren't really cousins were working the Saturday lunch shift while the rest of us took to the streets. As we approached, we could see the road blocked off with booths all around.

"How are customers supposed to get to La Cocina with this mess in the way?" Vanessa said.

We got closer, and Vanessa began handing out flyers. One guy standing nearby pulled out his wallet and gave her some cash.

"We don't want money, sir. Take this flyer, think about your neighborhood, and voice your concerns at the public forum in two weeks. Stand up for our community. Enjoy this commemorative La Cocina de la Isla cap!"

Vanessa gave another flyer to a woman eating festival food—shrimp sushi wrapped in lettuce. The woman said gracias, holding the flyer between her finger and the plate. We got to the lot to find the festival in full swing.

"What time did this thing start?" Brian asked.

"Eleven in the morning," Vanessa said, pointing to the sign. "It's going on until eight tonight."

There was a huge four-sided sign in front of the lot and our restaurant. It said EL FESTIVAL DE LAS ESTRELLAS on all four sides. The entire street parallel to the restaurant was blocked off from traffic and lined with little white booths. The lot itself was full of tents, with a large stage in the middle surrounded by lights, two large speakers, and a microphone stand. La Cocina was barely visible.

"Wow!" said a random guy wearing a too-tight shirt as he entered the festival. "Seriously, bro, this is legit!"

A little kid sculpted lumpy wads of sushi with his hand and stuffed his face.

An older couple fed each other and smiled as they savored the taste. Aunt Tuti looked around. "Where are they getting that food?"

Yolanda pointed at a tent where a sushi chef was carefully slicing sashimi into little squares and placing them on rice. There was already a huge line.

"He's making sushi right outside of our restaurant, Tía," Martín said, his large nostrils flaring up like a hippo before it attacks.

"This tent is taking away our business," my dad said.

We watched as a long line formed at the food tent. People left with long sticks with squares of fish on them.

"Is that even sanitary?" Mari asked. "Serving raw fish in public like that?"

"It is most sanitary, señorita," said a voice behind Mari.

Wilfrido Pipo was dressed in a lime-green suit with a red tie, and a hat covering his entire face. If it weren't for his bright smile, I wouldn't have recognized him. He tipped his hat and welcomed us.

"Ah, the famous Zamoras. And where is Doña Veronica?"

"She's not here."

"That's too bad. And your fearless leader, Chef Cari?"

"None of your concern. Oye, your free food is taking

away our business." Aunt Tuti tapped her foot so loudly, it sounded like conga drums.

"Oh? I didn't realize. Surely a few salmon rolls and yakitori skewers won't break the bank."

Uncle Carlos stood behind Aunt Tuti, his two sets of twins in a quadruple stroller. One of the kids got loose and asked someone walking by for a piece of salmon. He took a large bite. It looked like he immediately regretted his decision, because he made a face like he had just swallowed cardboard, and spit out the salmon onto the ground in front of everyone. Aunt Tuti laughed and walked over to pick up her nephew.

"Well, now we know the tackiness of your taste also affects your taste *buds*," she said.

Wilfrido shifted uncomfortably. He was outnumbered about fifteen to one.

"My tacky taste didn't keep you from stopping by to enjoy my free food and fun, did it?"

Vanessa pushed her way to the front and got up in Wilfrido's face. "We're not here to have fun," she said. "We're here to protest Pipo Place and the horrible things it would do to our community."

A growl escaped Wilfrido's throat, like a dog challenged to a fight. His left eye twitched and his face grew as red as the tie he was wearing.

"Listen here, little girl! All of you! I worked very hard to put on this event. I have tents full of free food and gifts that will seal the approval of this ridiculous family-friendly community. You will *not* stand in my way, do you hear? If I see one flyer or sign inside the festival, I will call the chief of police—someone I've gotten to know very well over the last few weeks. Face it—you are dinosaurs. And you know the beautiful thing about dinosaurs?" Wilfrido leaned in really close. So close, I could smell the soy sauce through his gritted pearly white teeth. "We know how big they once were by the bones they left behind. But that's all they are in this world now. Just bones."

Wilfrido tipped his hat and smiled at some people passing by to enter the festival. He threw a final icy stare at us before he disappeared into the crowd.

We were all speechless. He'd basically just called us extinct.

"¡Ja, no más!" Vanessa said, bringing us back to the present. "Like, seriously, we are Zamoras! Let's stop looking defeated and take some action!"

"You heard what he said, Vanessa. He'll call the police on us. I can't go to prison," Simon said as he tugged at his Green Teens shirt. "The debate team needs me!"

"We just have to change our plan a bit. Everyone, stay at the perimeter of the festival. No one actually goes inside," Vanessa said. "We have a right to be out here."

"She's right," Aunt Tuti said. "¡No somos dinosaurios! We can't give up now. Let's do it!"

"For Abuela," I said.

"For Abuela!" everyone shouted.

We stayed outside the festival grounds, but we made sure to talk to everyone heading in and out. Most people were happy to speak with us. Reminiscing about the restaurant and about Abuela. And some even admitted that they were only going in to collect the free gifts, but they did not really support Pipo Place. In that case, I couldn't blame them too much. The swag Wilfrido raffled off was pretty cool. Mini-speakers, iPads, more trips to the Caribbean. And even if you didn't win those, everyone left with water bottles, cell phone cases, hoodies, and Wilfrido's book about real estate. Okay, that last one wasn't cool, but I digress.

Carmen asked if she could be my protest partner, and I agreed even though I knew my stomach would be as twisted as a pretzel the whole time. She held a sign that said FAMILY IS COMMUNITY—COMMUNITY IS FAMILY while I passed out flyers.

"Isn't this so exciting?" she asked.

"Sure," I said.

"We're fighting for what we believe in. We're trying to make a difference, just like José Martí. He fought for Cuban independence from Spain. He wrote hundreds of essays on social justice, about the equal treatment of women, about the importance of children to the future of society, and about intellectual and social independence for the people of Latin America."

Whoa. How did she know all that?

"'Men of action, above all those whose actions are guided by love, live forever.' Oh, isn't that just beautiful? Martí wrote with passion, and it spilled out into his poetry and his life."

I knew José Martí was a poet, but I had no idea about the other stuff. I wondered if I had that kind of intellectual . . . whatever it was she said. I could hardly keep up with everything.

"Um, I believe in the equal treatment of women," I said, trying to say something important.

We spent the day protesting from behind our invisible barrier. Whenever there was a lull, Carmen told me more things about Martí. Like that he'd said, "We are free but not to be evil, not to be indifferent to human suffering," or something like that. She talked about how Martí charged up a hill in Cuba, a machete in his hand, demanding freedom for his people.

"He knew he was going to die," Carmen said, and I swore I saw a few tears drop from her eyes. "And yet he still charged because he knew, even in death, his work would live on." Carmen sighed. "It's so brave and romantic."

How the heck was I going to compete with a guy who wrote poetry, fought for the independence of an entire country, and died on the battlefield, fighting for freedom? And then I thought, wait a minute—why was I even getting jealous and why did I care so much and how was I ever going to prove myself to Carmen? If not for Aunt Tuti, I would have been lost in a vortex of jealousy and despair over a guy who had been dead for over a hundred years!

"Come inside," Aunt Tuti said, ushering everyone into the restaurant. "I'll make churros with crema de chocolate."

It seemed to cheer up the family a little. Aunt Tuti didn't cook much, but her churros were legendary.

"You all deserve it," she said, and began to prepare the deep-fried sugary sticks.

It was five o'clock, and the festival was still full of people enjoying themselves. La Cocina remained empty. At one point a couple popped in but then went back outside when they heard, "Free food all day!" from the loudspeakers.

After about thirty minutes Aunt Tuti brought out the homemade chocolate sauce and warm sugary churros. I took one and went to the dining room to eat.

Carmen waved me over, and I carefully balanced my churro and chocolate sauce as I sat next to her. She took a sip of water, then grabbed my hand and took a bite out of my churro.

"*So* delicious," she said, smiling.

I looked at my churro. If there was ever a moment to

declare you like someone, it was with a churro in your hand and a day of protesting a greedy land developer's hostile takeover of your neighborhood behind you. I was positive it was what Martí would have done. I thought of Abuelo's letter. Valor. Courage.

With sugary bits of churro stuck to the sides of my mouth, I started.

"Um, Carmen?"

"What's up?"

"Um, I, um." I dug into my pockets, forgetting about the churro in my hand. "I guess what I'm trying to say . . ."

"Yes?" she said as she watched me closely. It was like she waited for the greatest question to ever come out of a human being. It was then or never.

"Um, Carmen. I. Um. Like you. Like, I like you, like you. A lot. And, well, um, I was wondering if you, you know, you like me, maybe?"

There was a pause. A really uncomfortable pause. She took really long to say anything. My hands started to sweat. Her head moved slightly from side to side. A nervous smile crept onto her face. I breathed hard. Maybe too hard, because she leaned back a bit. Like she was trying to get away. I didn't know what to do. I backed away too. She didn't like me. Not that way, at least. I could tell. It felt like my stomach had turned into a vacuum cleaner to suck my chest into it.

"I'm sorry, Arturo. I . . . I can't. I'm not . . ." But she didn't finish her thought. She just made her way to the back of the restaurant without another word. I pushed away my plate of churros as I watched Carmen go outside. I stayed until I couldn't see her anymore. I stayed until I couldn't feel anything anymore. Carmen had quietly rejected me. Mop and Bren were wrong. Carmen didn't like me at all. And because I was sure I would forever associate churros with heartbreak, I knew that I'd probably never eat a churro again.

16

when the pot boils

I COULDN'T BELIEVE I had messed up so epically. I'd admitted I liked a girl, and it totally backfired. In my face! I paced around the restaurant while Brian munched on the last of his churro and Martín made jokes about the chocolate churros looking like poop. Martín was an imbecile. I went out to the patio and didn't see Carmen anywhere. She was probably avoiding me like I had the plague or something. Of course she didn't like me! She kept saying we were family. I should have known better. I could imagine myself talking to Abuelo.

"But, Abuelo, you said to have courage! To fight for your dreams, to fight for love like José Martí!"

"Yes, Arturito," he would say. "But you can't love

your mom's goddaughter like that! That's just wrong, dude."

Okay, maybe Abuelo wouldn't have said *dude*, but still! I had a view of the lot from the patio, and I could see Wilfrido Pipo onstage. He spoke excitedly into the microphone as festival-goers gathered.

It was almost eight and the sun had begun to drop over Main Street, casting shadows on the festival and turning the sky pink and orange. I thought of Pipo Place and the shadow it would cast if Wilfrido got his way. The building would absorb the entire neighborhood like a light-sucking vampire that turned everything into darkness.

"Good people, thank you all for coming to el Festival de las Estrellas! I hope you've all had a wonderful day."

I could have sworn Wilfrido winked at Commissioner García, who was standing in the front row. Dulce from Two Scoops was there as well. I also spotted Enrique and Ms. Patterson. Bicycle Bill sat on the outskirts of the growing crowd. He stroked his toy poodle, Henry, as he took in the scene. Was Wilfrido the Pied Piper or something?

"Look, everyone, this neighborhood is great. But don't you think it's time to take it to the next level?"

A few people clapped and nodded.

"It takes courage to embrace change," Wilfrido continued. "And I think you all have that. You really do."

I felt like he was stealing Abuelo's words. Courage wasn't something that Wilfrido had. My family had courage. Then I noticed Vanessa standing just outside of the festival, as Wilfrido had ordered, flyers limp in her hands. Ali stood by her. She dropped her head onto Vanessa's shoulder and wrapped her arm around her. It was like an admission of defeat. It was a we-did-our-best kind of gesture. I could see flyers scattered in the streets just a few feet behind them, left behind by people who were now enjoying the festival.

I looked back at my family. Uncle Carlos pushed the quadruple stroller back and forth, trying to put his four kids to sleep. Aunt Tuti watched quietly and reached for Uncle Carlos's hand. He took it in the way a younger brother takes the hand of his older sister when he wants things to be okay. My family gathered closer together, confined to our patio. I looked at Wilfrido onstage. Alone.

This ridiculous family-friendly coummunity, he had said.

Where was Wilfrido's family? All that success, and I never heard him talk about anyone who he cared about. Not one person. That was when it all clicked into place for me. All the towns where Wilfrido had developed land were tight-knit communities. Just like Canal Grove.

I looked at the crowd again. Annabelle and George held hands while they listened to Wilfrido. They had known each other since middle school. The same Palm

Middle that I went to. They were getting married where Annabelle's parents had gotten married years before. Ms. Patterson and Ms. Minerva had worked at the same school for over thirty years. Dulce started Two Scoops a year after La Cocina opened. Enrique was a prodigy at Palm High, left to attend a top art school in Paris, and returned to his hometown to open a gallery. Bicycle Bill . . . well, nobody really knew where Bicycle Bill came from, but he had lived in the neighborhood for as long as anybody could remember!

"It's time to usher in a new era!" Wilfrido yelled. "Where money will flow from the buildings that rise!"

Something suddenly came over me. I grabbed the sign Carmen had held earlier and marched toward the stage. I lifted the sign over my head and walked through the crowd, showing them all what they failed to see for themselves.

FAMILY IS COMMUNITY—COMMUNITY IS FAMILY

"This community is about family! Canal Grove has always been about family. And now you want this guy who knows nothing about us to come in here and mess with our family?"

"Hey!" Wilfrido yelled. "You're not supposed to have that on festival grounds!"

Wilfrido's security reached out for me, but before they could grab me, I swung the sign like a weapon and sprang back.

"Get him out of here!" Wilfrido yelled. He ordered more security to come after me, but I swung my poster around like a sword to ward them off. Before I could do anything, I felt my sign ripped out of my hands from above. The security guards stopped, and when I looked up, I saw Wilfrido had plucked my sign from his post on the stage. His face had turned so red, he looked like a crab that had been boiled so long, its claws were about to crack. He was disgusted by the sign.

"Community is family? I'll show you what family is."

Wilfrido snapped the sign in half with his knee and tossed the broken bits into the crowd. A few people ducked and scattered out of the way.

"Family is a flawed system. Family will not save you or provide for you or keep you safe. The only thing that keeps you safe is money. Do you think these people care about your family, little boy? They don't. They care about themselves. Do you think Chuchi isn't beaming at the prospect of a whole new flock of business once my building goes up? Do you think the commissioner isn't jumping for joy, knowing by the time elections come around, he will have presided over the biggest economic growth this town has ever seen? You think because people go to your restaurant that they owe you some kind of allegiance?"

"You're wrong!" I yelled, storming the stage. "Just because *you* don't have a family, or don't care about them, doesn't mean *they* don't care about theirs." I pointed to everyone in the crowd.

"You be quiet about my family, little boy."

"Why don't you ever talk about your family? What are you hiding?" I yelled at the top of my lungs while Wilfrido gritted his teeth and tried to smile at the crowd.

"Family is a competition where the strongest gets the inheritance. *That* is how success is taught." Wilfrido sneered, then drew in close. His breath smelled like room-temperature cheese. "I beat my family and my brothers and sisters and earned my father's love. You win by being strong. Not sentimental and weak."

Wilfrido stepped away from me and addressed the crowd.

"This boy and his family are beginning to look like sore losers!" Wilfrido laughed and continued. "They are sneaking around, trying to rally and protest something that is perfectly within my right to do. Apparently, your abuela and abuelo didn't learn that in *this* country, people are free to buy property."

"They knew that," I said, my voice loud and bold. "But José Martí said, 'We are free.'" I tried to remember the quote Carmen said. "'But not to be indifferent,' um, 'indifferent,' from the . . . Darn, what did he say?"

"You can't even remember the quote! Pathetic!"

"'But not to profit from the people, from the work created and sustained through their spirit,'" Bicycle Bill chimed in as he walked to the foot of the stage. He slowly picked up the broken sign and took it back to his bike.

"Whatever the quote, this is my festival, and I have done nothing wrong by placing a bid on this property. And *you* have intruded and handed out propaganda when I explicitly told you not to. Now, get this boy out of my sight!"

Everyone in the crowd looked like they had just seen an alien spaceship land. Their jaws were on the floor. Before I could figure out what that meant, I felt two hands grab me and escort me off the stage.

"Don't touch my nephew!" Aunt Tuti yelled at Wilfrido's festival security guards. On my way to wherever they were taking me, I caught a glimpse of Carmen on the restaurant's patio. I guess she'd seen the whole thing. It felt like a thousand pounds of refried beans had just been dumped onto my head.

17

words you never want to hear

THE FESTIVAL HOLDING cell was a mobile office with three rooms closed off from one another that ran the length of the trailer. From the way it creaked and smelled, it was probably brand-new fifty years ago. It felt like being in a rectangular lunch box floating on the ocean.

On the window, a palmetto bug looked like it was trying to decide if it wanted to snoop around the dirty streets or stay put. I scooted away from it because palmetto bugs looked like mutant roaches, and even though they didn't bite, they were still freakishly big. It would probably find the half-eaten churro that had fallen out of my pocket and feast on its sugary heartbreak.

Outside the window, Wilfrido's team took down tents and booths, so I had a clear view of La Cocina—a reminder of my failed attempt to convince the neighborhood that the restaurant belonged. By now my family was probably at the apartment. Ya se acabó. It was all over.

I could feel the trailer sway from side to side, as if a stampede of rhinos marched down the narrow aisle. Angry voices got closer and closer, and suddenly the latch to my cell shook until it finally unhinged and the door swung open. Aunt Tuti marched inside like an alligator ready to snap.

She turned around and took a defensive stance against the other people storming into my tiny cell. It was Wilfrido and a police officer.

"Do you think that you can come onto *my* stage and ruin *my* festival?!" Wilfrido said, pointing at me. But the trailer rocked so much, he had to hold himself up against the roof with both hands to prevent himself from falling.

"Am I going to be arrested?" I asked the police officer standing behind him.

"Nobody's arresting anybody, Arturo," Aunt Tuti said, squeezing past Wilfrido.

"¡Señora! careful with my hair." Wilfrido checked his coif and slithered out of the cell like the snake he was.

"My nephew was exercising freedom of speech. That is not a crime. Right, Rogelio?"

"He's free to go," Officer Rogelio said, and Aunt Tuti patted him affectionately on the back.

"Thanks," she said, and we moved across the street.

"Anytime," Officer Rogelio replied.

Wilfrido stepped out of the trailer.

"You're lucky the police chief wasn't available to take my call, niño travieso."

Aunt Tuti lunged at him, but Officer Rogelio held her back while Wilfrido adjusted his suit and sauntered away. I wanted to run after Wilfrido. I wanted to dump a pot of lard all over his head and his stupid festival and his Pipo Place.

"Can you believe this guy, Aunt Tuti?" I said, turning around, my blood still boiling. Aunt Tuti stared quietly at her phone. Her eyes welled with tears that began streaming down her face, mixing with her makeup to make black streaks.

"Aunt Tuti?" I asked, but she didn't answer.

She remained frozen for a moment, staring at her screen before whispering, "It's Abuela, Arturo. She's been taken to the hospital."

"But she's okay? Right?"

Aunt Tuti typed on her phone. Something was wrong with my ears, because it was like all other sounds were blocked except for her phone dinging very loudly.

"I don't know, mi amor. Come on. Let's get home."

We walked in silence. The streets were empty except

for a few trucks that had come to take the festival tents away. There were massive amounts of garbage all over the ground. I wondered who was going to pick up all that mess. I knew it wasn't going to be Wilfrido Pipo. The entire way home, my chest thumped like a volcano ready to erupt.

Aunt Tuti walked me all the way inside when we finally got to the complex.

"It'll be okay, honey. Don't worry."

Tuti hadn't called me honey since I was a little kid. She pulled me in and hugged me tightly. I didn't mind it so much, because she smelled like plums, and she felt squishy and soft when you hugged her. One of the stones from her necklace poked me in the eye and I pulled away.

"¡Ay, pobrecito! Poor thing! Ven, let me see."

Tuti licked her thumb and wiped the corner of my eye.

"You have a moco in your ojito."

I pulled back. My mother would have *never* done that.

"Don't tell your mom, okay? She hates it when I clean you like that. Vieja presumida." Tuti was right. If my mom had seen her doing it, she would probably have tightened her lips and, without her saying a word, everyone would have known how displeased she was.

"Okay, mi amor. Your mom said there's some picadillo in the kitchen. Tus padres won't be back until later tonight. Eat, okay? Estás muy flaquito."

I wasn't *really* skinny. I just wasn't big-boned. Tuti must have taken after Abuelo. Abuelo was short and round. Abuela was tall and lean with very thin wrists and long arms that wrapped all the way around when she hugged.

"Don't forget to eat, honey."

Tuti gave me a kiss and left. In the kitchen I saw the big plate of picadillo with rice and black beans. There was enough food on the plate to feed me for six days. I wasn't really hungry, so I put it away.

I learned that my mom had gone into Abuela's apartment and found her lying peacefully in bed, but when she didn't respond, my mom knew something was wrong. I imagined Abuela with tubes and monitors strapped all over her body. I wanted to go visit, but Aunt Tuti said it was better if I stayed. Abuela was at the hospital again. The last thing I wanted was to be alone in my house.

A few hours passed, and I couldn't concentrate. I went to my desk and opened Abuelo's box. I emptied it until my desk was completely covered. I sifted through the papers and pulled out the CD.

Guantanamera.

I loaded the CD into my computer. But before I could click on the song, my mom knocked on the door and slowly walked into the room. She never knocked. Her lips weren't pursed in the way they got when she was focused. They were droopy, like they were tired of moving. She took a few seconds to speak, and the thump in my chest slowly began to fill the quiet.

"Arturo," she said, her eyes steady on mine. She stood next to me as I continued to sit at my desk. Even sitting, I was almost taller than her.

"Arturo?"

I remained quiet until finally she broke our silence. "I'm sorry, mijo, but your abuela passed away tonight."

And at that, my heart started racing uncontrollably.

"Your father will make the arrangements your abuela requested tomorrow. We've decided, as a family, that we will all attend Sunday mass tomorrow morning, and we will ask the priest to pray for Abuela. The restaurant will be closed all of next week, and we will have a memorial dinner at the restaurant next Sunday. Get some rest. We have a lot of things to prepare."

She walked out, went into her bedroom, and closed the door. Music crackled from my speakers. I had forgotten that I'd cued up a song. I recognized the words sung by the chorus. These were the same words used in the José Martí poem that I had read in Carmen's book, in Abuelo's letters, in Abuela's book. They were all the same.

Cultivo una rosa blanca
I cultivate a white rose

En junio como en enero,
In June like in January,

Para el amigo sincero
For my sincere friend

Que me da su mano franca.
Who gives me his honest hand.

¡Guantanamera! Guajira, Guantanamera.
Guantanamera! Guajira, Guantanamera.

¡Guantanamera! Guajira, Guantanamera.
Guantanamera! Guajira, Guantanamera.

The song finished, and I wanted to shut down my computer and run away. Run away and try to beat the hurt that was chasing me. But I didn't. I clicked on it again—because I recognized it—and I read the lyrics again—because I knew them. Then I listened to the song again, and then again. Repeating quietly to myself: *I failed. I failed. I failed.*

Dear reader, I told you not to be fooled by high expectations. You could have a plan. You could organize and have courage and work and try to make a change. But the only thing that counted in the end was the result. I'd thought I could save the restaurant and tell Carmen I liked her. But instead I'd gotten an arrow through my heart, and I was pretty sure we were going to lose La Cocina, our second home. And on top of all that—I'd lost Abuela. There was no happy ending to my story. Punto. Final.

TOTAL. EPiC. FAiL.

The song continued to play, and I fell asleep, my face planted on the keyboard.

18

write here

I WOKE UP in the middle of the night, tucked Abuelo's box under my arm, and snuck out of my apartment. To Abuela's. My stomach sank as I walked past her old KitchenAid blender. I'd probably never be able to drink a mango batido again. Abuela's dark-red curtains blocked out the light from the security lamp in the courtyard. The room was hot, and my stomach sank a little deeper. Abuela would never have let it get so hot in her apartment. AC was the one luxury she didn't mind spending money on. She'd never had that in Cuba and thought it was a marvel.

What an incredible invention! she'd said. *To have winter in your home and year-round summer outside.*

I looked over at Abuela's couch, which was covered in plastic. For some reason, Abuela felt that lining the cushions with plastic was the best way to preserve them. That meant that you couldn't sit on her sofa if you were wearing shorts because the plastic would stick to the back of your legs, and even if you didn't have a lot of hair like me, the little you had would rip off and cause all kinds of irritation.

Her recliner was next to the sofa. She got the recliner secondhand, so it wasn't covered in plastic, which meant it had conformed to her shape. I thought about the last time I'd come over. I'd read her that poem. The poem that hadn't escaped my mind all night. The poem printed in the book resting inside a fruit bowl on top of her coffee table. *Versos sencillos* por José Martí.

"Abuela, why did Wilfrido Pipo come to our neighborhood? Why do some people seem to be on his side?"

Háblame en español, mi amor. She would always remind me to speak to her in Spanish. *Practice,* she'd say. I didn't speak it very well even though I understood most things. I'd gotten better, but only a little.

I imagined Abuela saying people act like that because their centers are mixed incorrectly—like a sauce that curdles from overheating. You have to be even-tempered and not whisk yourself up too much.

I plucked the book from the fruit bowl and flipped to the end. It said:

Todo es hermoso y constante,

Todo es música y razón,

Y todo, como el diamante,

Antes que luz es carbón.

The last lines of the poem said that before becoming a diamond, everything was first coal. But nothing had turned into a diamond. Nothing was the success it was supposed to be. Abuela would have the answers, but she was gone. She'd been too sick. Maybe I'd stressed her out. Now everything was ruined. It was my fault. Abuela was gone.

The truth finally hit me. Abuela had died. I fell onto her couch. I desperately wanted the cushions to absorb me and swallow me whole. But instead the plastic cover squeaked, like it was trying to make sense of me sitting down on it. I fought back tears by opening Abuelo's box and looking through the letters. I took one out and read the envelope.

A VECES LO TIENES QUE ESCRIBIR

SOMETIMES YOU NEED
TO WRITE IT DOWN

The letter inside was blank.

"What am I supposed to do with a blank page, Abuelo?" I asked out loud.

There were stacks of blank pages with the words *WRITE HERE* written across the top.

"What am I going to write, Abuelo?" I wasn't a writer. I didn't have any idea what to put down. I looked through the box and tried to find another letter. Maybe there was something else Abuelo had left that could give me advice. A pen fell out and landed on my foot as I dug through the box. I glanced back at the blank pages next to me.

WRITE HERE

"Okay, okay. But I can't promise it will be good." I shook the pen a few times to get the ink going, and placed a blank page on top of Abuela's coffee table. Before I started writing, I went to the thermostat and blasted the AC to sixty-five degrees. The machine grumbled to life, and soon Abuela's apartment felt like it should.

I stared at the blank page, closed my eyes, opened them again, and began to write.

I wrote for hours. I wrote until the pen cracked and ink dripped everywhere and made a mess of my words on the page. I wrote through blank page after blank page. About the moment I was thrown into the festival holding cell. About our Sunday family dinners. About

Mop and Bren and how much I wished they were here. About Carmen and how I hoped she'd still want to be my friend after what had happened. About my family. My crazy family! About Abuela and Abuelo—how I hoped they were reunited. About what our final days at the restaurant would be like if we lost it. I scribbled fast and long, sometimes not even thinking about what I wrote before I wrote it. I remembered every detail of the past few weeks.

I wrote until I passed out on Abuela's sofa, a bed of papers underneath me.

In the morning, I woke to the sound of my name echoing in my ear. I opened one eye to find my mom standing over me.

"There you are, Arturo. Your father and I have been looking for you," she said, and began organizing the papers spread all over the place.

I looked at the stack of pages I had composed. *WRITE HERE.*

19

the last batido

I SHOWERED QUICKLY, changed, and met the family in the courtyard. They all looked like they hadn't slept at all. Brian and Martín shuffled in slowly while Vanessa slouched in the corner. It was the first time she wasn't front and center. I don't know if it was the shower or the feeling of release I had from writing all night, but I was happy to see them. My family.

"Okay, everyone," my mom began. "We all know the city council will vote on the bids in ten days. Whatever the outcome, let's use this week to be together and honor Abuela. Let's go to the beach, let's see a movie, let's dip our feet in the canals or go for a walk. Do everything that Abuela loved. Enjoy everything that made her happy."

"Can we take Carlos's truck and ram Pipo's office? That would make *me* happy," Aunt Tuti blurted out between sobs.

"No, Tuti, we're not doing that," my mom continued. "I don't want to think about that man or the bids. I want to stay positive."

"Positive?" Aunt Tuti sobbed. "Positive?"

"Yes," my mom said. "Win or lose. Now let's think about other things."

The family completely ignored my mom's request and chattered among themselves about what would happen if Wilfrido won the vote.

"I refuse to believe he'll win. We can't think like that!"

"Yeah, the neighborhood can't possibly be on that guy's side!"

"It sure looked like a bunch of people were on his side at the festival," Mari said.

"But they took our flyers," Martín replied.

"They were scattered all over the street," Vanessa said.

"What has happened to this neighborhood?"

"It's like they're under a spell or something!"

"Wilfrido has enchanted them!"

"Maybe we should protest at city hall, too. I can get my team on it," Vanessa offered.

"That's a great idea, Vanessa, but no," my mom said.

"I can't believe you're giving up, Cari!"

"I'm not giving up, Tuti. I'm thinking of our family."

"That's not what Mami would have wanted! She would have fought."

"Mami isn't here, Tuti. It's only us."

My mom and Aunt Tuti argued back and forth, which made everyone else get really quiet. My mom's cheeks turned bright red. Aunt Tuti's face tightened as if to hold back tears, but the tears splashed out anyway. I felt a nervous energy all around, and I tried to think of a way to stop them, but no words came out.

Abuela's absence was so strong, it literally broke us. If she were here, all she'd have to do was take our hands and offer a prayer and everyone would quiet down and listen. Instead I watched my family crack open. Finally my mom put an end to the conversation.

"Mami made me the principal owner of this restaurant, and I am going to do what is best for this family."

I looked around, and everyone tried to avoid eye contact with my mom. When I finally met her gaze, she had the look on her face that she'd give the cooks who didn't listen to her in the kitchen.

"We need to stop this emotional runaround. Abuela is gone! We've been so focused on losing that we've forgotten what is important, and that is family. If we lose, and our lease isn't renewed, we'll find a new location. But that's enough fighting. No more."

"No," I said. I realized I was the only one speaking

now. The whole family had gone quiet. Even Tuti had retreated to a bench.

"Mom, we can't give up. We have to keep fighting."

My dad came up to my mom. He was always the calm one of the family. I had never heard him yell or scream at anyone. It was why he was so good at customer service at the restaurant. Even if a guest was rude, my dad never lost his temper.

"Cari," he said. "Remember that this restaurant is what your parents built their whole lives on. It isn't just a building—it's a home. *We* built our whole lives on it too. I think that's what Arturo's trying to say."

"I know, Robert, but we need to stop trying to change things that are not in our control."

A lump formed in my throat, and I found it hard to swallow.

"But . . . Abuela . . ." I could hardly manage.

"Arturo," my mom said, her voice softer now, almost like she was trying to whisper. "Abuela and Abuelo left a place many years ago and found a new home—a new life. They made new memories and kept their old ones in their hearts."

I turned away from her. What was stopping someone like Wilfrido Pipo from chasing down another neighborhood and building *another* high-rise? And then moving to *another* neighborhood and building another? And then another? He had done it before.

"Arturo?"

I had my mother's eyes, dark and round. But I had my father's height. I was already a head taller than her. I didn't nod or shake my head. The neighborhood didn't really want Pipo Place. They just liked his free gifts and flashy parties. I saw Carmen appear from behind Abuela's floribunda bush, and I turned away so our eyes wouldn't meet. I suddenly felt like being alone, and I turned to leave. Some of my family members looked like they wanted to talk to me, but I just couldn't deal with it.

I went to our apartment and then my room and shut the door. My mom called out a few minutes later, but I didn't answer. No more conversations. I thought about how things could change so quickly. A few weeks ago Mop and Bren were still here, Carmen wasn't around yet to confuse me, the restaurant was safe, and Abuela was still . . . well, anyway.

I checked my computer to see if I had any Twitter messages from Bren. He hadn't called or texted in a while. I sent him a message just as my dad knocked on the door.

"Mind if I come in?"

He opened it slowly and popped his head in. I nodded, and the rest of his body came out from behind the door. He handed me a huge bowl of mint chocolate chip ice cream, winked at me, and slipped back out. My dad was really cool like that.

I kicked off my sneakers and reclined on my bed, trying to keep the bowl of ice cream from tipping over. It almost did when I heard a ding from my computer. Bren had sent me a message, so I put the bowl down on my desk and went to read it.

@PITBULL4LIF: how's it goin over there, dude?

I thought about telling Bren that Abuela had passed away, but it felt like something I should say in person. Plus, I really just wanted to feel normal for a second—like nothing had changed.

@ARTZAM3: hey, bren, not that good. what's up with you?

@PITBULL4LIF: had a gf for a bit. didn't work out. don't understand women. how's carmen? u guys make out yet?

@ARTZAM3: totally not happening.

@PITBULL4LIF: give love a chance, bro. so what's the deal with the restaurant stuff?

@ARTZAM3: i think wilfrido pipo's going to win and my family has given up.

@PITBULL4LIF: dude, u better not give up!!!

@ARTZAM3: it seems like a fight that's impossible to win, u know?

@PITBULL4LIF: u. are. arturo freakin zamora! u practiced and practiced to get on the bball team, and after tryouts coach was so impressed, he let you on.

@ARTZAM3: i was on the practice team, dude.

@PITBULL4LIF: bro, u got a jersey and became the first sixth grader to ever play on the eighth-grade team!!! instant popularity upgrade.

@ARTZAM3: yeah, i guess. hey, i wrote some poetry.

I waited for Bren to answer. Finally, he responded in a not-so-subtle way..

@PITBULL4LIF: WHAT?!!!!!

@ARTZAM3: yeah, I know. weird, huh?

@PITBULL4LIF: have u shown anyone?

@ARTZAM3: r u crazy?!

@PITBULL4LIF: just sayin. u know carmen would dig it.

@ARTZAM3: definitely not, dude.

@PITBULL4LIF: worth a try. dang! dude, gotta go. my mom is yelling at me to stop sitting on the couch in my wet shorts. don't give up!

@ARTZAM3: k. talk to you l8er. hey, bren?

@PITBULL4LIF: what up, compadre?

@ARTZAM3: thanks, dude.

@PITBULL4LIF: no problem. l8er, bro.

Bren signed out. My ice cream had completely melted in the bowl, so I slurped up the minty liquid left behind. It tasted like a milk shake. It tasted like a batido. Abuela's batido.

20

eating in silence

WE ALL ATTENDED regular mass and then Father Samuel held an additional special service just for Abuela at the end. As people filed out after normal mass, Father Samuel asked us to move up to the first few rows of benches.

"She was a beacon in this community and this parish," Father Samuel said. "It is a privilege to honor her today."

That's the kind of impact Abuela had. A priest would make an exception for her.

I looked around at the family, Carmen and her dad, and Mop's parents. We didn't invite more people to stay because my mom wanted to keep it small and intimate. She placed a bouquet of flowers on the altar along with a framed picture of Abuela smiling.

Uncle Carlos rubbed his forehead and pushed the quadruple stroller quietly in the aisle. The two sets of twins had fallen asleep peacefully. Brian wore his sunglasses inside the church, and Martín just kept his head down. Aunt Tuti was real quiet but would let out occasional shrieks and wails so loud, the next church three miles away could have heard her. My dad held my mom's hand and never took his eyes off Abuela's picture.

My mom's lips were so tightly pressed together, they could have easily been one lip. I didn't think she even blinked.

I stared at Abuela's photo. It felt weird seeing her picture there. She was going to be cremated in two days, as soon as all the paperwork was complete. A body of ashes trapped in a vase forever. I hated the thought of Abuela trapped anywhere.

There was a single white rose in the middle of all the other colorful flowers. I don't know if anyone else noticed, but I saw it. White roses were Abuela's favorite. I imagined for a second that rose was for me. That it was for my eyes only.

Cultivo una rosa blanca

That was what the poem said. The translation was: *I cultivate a white rose.* All I could think about was how Abuela had gardened. And how she had cooked. And how, before she'd gotten sick, she'd read stories to me. And how those stories had been shared with Abuelo, her lifelong love. They were stories of heroes and poets and love and sacrifice. Of leaving your country for another. Of learning that family is the only home worth claiming. Their stories always had love in them. Abuelo's letters showed me that.

The white rose on her coffin reminded me of everything I had and everything I had lost. My whole world felt like it was slipping away.

Aunt Tuti spoke first, and then I was supposed to say a few words on behalf of the grandkids. But when I thought of the urn filled with Abuela's ashes and Aunt Tuti crying and my mom's stone face and everyone else sniffling and rubbing their eyes, I decided not to. I just couldn't do it, and I guess that wasn't good, because I missed my chance to tell everyone what Abuela meant to me. Then it was my mom's turn to speak.

"In light of Abuela's passing," she began, "we are going to have a memorial dinner at the restaurant next Sunday. If you can, please let our customers know that next Sunday's family dinner will be open to everyone."

My mom talked about Abuela's commitment to the neighborhood and to the families who lived here.

"It's what she would have wanted," my mom concluded.

When our special mass was over, I saw Mop's mom and dad. They saw me too and came over.

"I know Mop wishes he were here, Arturo."

"Yeah, I wish he were too," I said.

"Hey, you let us know if you need anything," Mop's dad said.

"Thanks." I appreciated that Mop's parents hadn't gone to Wilfrido Pipo's dumb festival.

"And we'll be at the restaurant next week," Mop's mom said. "We're going to bring a few other friends who knew Abuela. We'll try to get Mop down here as well."

"Cool," I said.

My family walked together through the streets, back to the apartment complex. But slowly, we split up. Yolanda and Mari left to post information about Abuela's memorial dinner near the restaurant. Brian called people on the phone and my dad sent e-mails. It was obvious that we weren't having Sunday family dinner tonight. I tried to think of another time when dinner was canceled, but I couldn't come up with anything. I walked alone until my mom caught up to me.

"Arturo?" she asked. "I'd like for you to cook Abuela's memorial dinner with me next week."

My mom stared at me with her intense brown eyes. She wasn't playing. She really wanted me to cook with her.

"What about Martín?" I asked, thinking that was a way better idea.

"I'd like some time alone with you," she said, walking ahead. "We'll go to the restaurant tomorrow and think of the menu to prepare for Abuela's dinner."

"Um? I thought we were going to chill and honor Abuela this week?"

"This is how you and I will honor her. By cooking together."

She disappeared into our apartment. My mom wanted me to cook with her?

Out of the corner of my eye I saw Carmen coming up to me, and I panicked. We hadn't really spoken since my total epic fail at the protest.

"How are you feeling, Arturo?"

"Well, we just got out of Abuela's funeral mass, so . . . not great." I knew it sounded mean as the words were coming out, but I couldn't stop them.

"Yeah, of course. That was a stupid question. Almost as stupid as when one of my dad's friends asked if I missed my mom two days after her funeral."

I suddenly remembered that Carmen had lost her mother not too long ago. That was the whole reason she was here for the summer. I felt like a complete jerk.

"Hey, I'm sorry for snapping. I didn't get much sleep last night," I said, and yawned really loudly. I left out the part about writing.

"Don't worry about it; I understand," she said while looking at her shoes like they were the most fascinating things in the world. "By the way, have you seen my book of poetry?" she asked. "I've been looking for it everywhere, and I could really use some versos sencillos right now."

"Huh? Oh, um, no," I said, because I had forgotten to give it back to her and didn't want her to think I'd had it all this time without telling her. "Maybe you left it somewhere. But if you really want to read it, Abuela has an old edition. We can go check if you want?"

"Okay," she said, smiling as she followed me to Abuela's apartment.

We walked in, and the AC was still on. The coolness gave me goose bumps, but I didn't mind. Abuela's copy of the Martí book was still on the coffee table.

"Here it is," I said, handing it to her.

"That's awesome," she said. "Look how old the book is!"

"Keep it," I said. Did I really mean that? I decided I did.

"I can't keep this," she said. "No way."

"She would have wanted you to have it."

Carmen opened the book to the first few pages and started reading silently.

She shook her head. "I won't keep it," she said. "It's too special."

"Well, at least borrow it."

Carmen paced around the room, reading while I dug

through a bunch of Abuela's old photographs. I thought people at the memorial might want to see some. There was one with Abuela and Abuelo on a beach. Uncle Carlos was in Abuela's arms, and my mom held on to Abuelo's hand while Aunt Tuti showed off her missing two front teeth with a smile.

Some pictures were slightly torn around the edges, and others were taken in a time when cars looked like round, colorful toasters. Abuela stood in front of a car like that, wearing white pants and a flowing jacket. Her hair was really short and curly, and even though the picture was black-and-white, you could see her bright eyes glowing.

Carmen kept reading as I flipped through the pictures. Neither one of us said a word. Occasionally Carmen made a comment about how it seemed like José Martí could be read in any time period.

"His poetry is political but full of love and hope," she said, and I nodded. But really, I had no idea what she was talking about.

"Hey, check this out," I said. "Who does this look like?"

Carmen put down Abuela's book of poems and stared at the black-and-white photo.

"It looks just like José Martí!" she said.

"It can't be," I said. "Martí died, like, more than a hundred years ago."

"Well, yes, but the building La Cocina is in is really

old," Carmen said. "He could have stopped there to give a speech or something."

"Hang on," I said, checking my phone for reference. I typed the address of La Cocina and added *historical* to the search. Nothing came up. I typed, *José Martí and La Cocina de la Isla*, but still nothing came up. Then I typed *Merritt family and José Martí*, since the Merritts' ancestors practically founded this town, and a few hits popped up about the late 1800s.

"The Merritt family is one of the oldest families in the neighborhood," I told Carmen. "And look—some of the original Merritts might have had a connection to Martí."

"So how does that help us?" Carmen asked, getting closer.

"Abuela used to work for the descendants of the Merritts. It's possible there is a link somehow."

"Maybe that's why she has this photo!" she said, jumping up. "And if the building La Cocina is located in is actually *historical* . . . ?"

"It can't be torn down."

Carmen jumped up and down excitedly. "How can we find out for sure?"

We left Abuela's apartment, taking the old photo of Cuba's most famous hero with us. When we got to the courtyard, we ran into my mom, who sat waiting on a bench.

"What's up?" she asked.

"Mom, we found something."

"If this is about Wilfrido, I don't want to hear it."

"It's not. It's about the . . ."

"Arturo"—my mom shot both of us a look—"I don't want to hear it right now. Okay?"

Carmen placed her hand on my shoulder, and that rumbling, stiff-throat, nervous-like-a-fish-being-reeled-in feeling came back. I shrugged it off. Carmen didn't like me like that.

My mom got up and made her way back to the apartment. She took slow steps up the stairs, and I could tell she was tired. I decided to leave her alone.

Uncle Frank saw us through his window and came out to give me a hug.

"You really have grown, Arturo."

Uncle Frank was super tall. I may have grown, but I felt like a little kid in his arms.

"Mi amor, can you help me with the website? I forgot what I needed to do to post something with photographs. And a little girl from Andalucía sent a comment. Can you respond to her?"

Carmen and Uncle Frank had been working on a blog for kids who had lost a parent to sickness. It was mostly in Spanish, and the site had nice pictures on it. The front page had a picture of Carmen's mom, with a caption about her story. Carmen had put in a comment section for people to send questions or share their stories.

"Okay, Papá," she said. "See you later, Arturo?"

I nodded and watched as she walked with Uncle Frank back to her apartment. She stopped, told her dad something, and ran back to me.

"Hey," she said with a sad kind of smile. Her shiny braces made little red and blue sparkles on her teeth. "It gets better, you know? Losing someone."

I watched as the words slowly came out of her mouth. Something about Carmen's smile made me, I dunno, less mad at things.

My parents were on the sofa when I got home, sitting in the silence. I think I startled them, because my mom flinched a little when she lifted her head off my dad's shoulder. Her eyes were puffy, and she kept blowing her nose. She tried to smile at me, but she didn't say anything. My dad smiled and winked. He had a way of lightening even the saddest moments. He caressed my mom's head as she lowered it back onto his shoulder.

My mom had just returned to Miami after working for a few years in fancy New York City restaurants when she'd met my dad. He was in town from Los

Angeles, where he acted in commercials. He stopped at Lola's Café on the far side of Main Street for a coffee one day. That was where, from what my dad tells me, things didn't start out that great.

"I spent the entire morning apologizing to your mother for having spilled coffee all over her white chef coat. She finally agreed to let me buy her another one, and the rest is history."

"That's how he remembers it," my mom would always say. "It was more like, he followed me all the way to La Cocina, begging me to accept a new coffee."

"Which she did."

Every time my parents told this story, they each had their version of how it went down. And it often prompted playful bickering. It was the way they expressed their love. Abuelo and Abuela expressed theirs differently. I guess the common thread was that both my abuelo and my dad kind of failed epically the first time they'd met Abuela and my mom.

I went up to my room and checked to see if Bren was online. And I hoped Mop would be able to come to the memorial dinner next Sunday.

When I didn't hear from Bren, I checked the family group chat. There weren't any conversations. It was the first time that had ever happened. Someone always sent at least a funny picture or a viral video. It felt weird to not talk to my family on a Sunday. I looked at the photograph of Martí again and put it away. Now wasn't the time to be an activist or a poet or any of those things. I took out Abuelo's box and looked at the remaining blank pages. They reminded me of silence. Silence was another way to remember.

21

memory games

THE NEXT MORNING, my mom came in to wake me up before my Hulk alarm went off.

"Up, up, up," she said, but I just rolled over and buried my head in the sheets. "Arturo, vamos. I want to get to the restaurant and make a list of the things we need to buy."

"But you said we should take this week to chill." I popped my head out momentarily while my mom tapped my leg.

"Yes, and one of the things Abuela would have wanted was for you and me to cook a wonderful meal together for the entire community. So, we need to plan."

I dragged myself out of bed.

"Here," my mom said, handing me a chef coat. "Abuela had this made for you."

The coat had my initials on it.

"When did Abuela do this?"

"I told her I wasn't sure if you wanted to cook or that you were even ready yet. But you know your abuela—stubborn and insistent."

She was right, and that made me smile.

I got ready and followed my mom into the kitchen. My dad handed us two egg sandwiches and gave my mom a to-go cup of what smelled like café con leche.

"Can I get one of those?" I asked, because there's nothing better than sweet Cuban coffee with warm condensed milk in the morning. It's like regular coffee's fun-loving cousin.

My dad raised his eyebrow at me as he slid another to-go cup across the counter. I sipped it, and my senses heightened. Ahhh. Yes, I was ready for the day.

When we arrived at the restaurant, my mom got out of the car to place a black bow on the door.

"Un crespón," she said, tying it around one of the handles. "It's how businesses remember the departed."

We put up a sign outside saying that Abuela had passed away. Reading it made me feel as horrible as when my mom had come into my room to tell me right after it had happened.

We got back into the car, and Mom motioned for me to take out the notepad and pencil she always kept in the glove compartment, so I could take notes as she dictated the menu. We went to every local farm and vendor and ordered all kinds of fresh ingredients. Every place we visited had the same reaction to the news about Abuela.

Manny, the farmer we bought our fruits and vegetables from, held my mom for, like, ten minutes. He gave us all the produce we needed and didn't charge us.

"I will be there on Sunday, Doña Caridad. With my children and grandchildren."

Manny wasn't the only one who contributed to Abuela's memorial dinner. Alfredo and Melinda Ortega, our butchers, gave us all the chicken, beef, and pork my dad's pickup truck could carry. And then they followed us to the restaurant and delivered more.

"Doña Veronica was the first restaurant who picked our humble farm over the larger chains. The gratitude we have for her can never be repaid."

It was amazing to see an entirely different group of people express their love, sadness, and appreciation for Abuela. I never thought about the farms and businesses the restaurant bought supplies from and the people who owned those businesses.

"She didn't care that it was a little more expensive,"

my mom told me. "She wanted to support her neighbors. Your abuela was ahead of the game. She invented farm-to-table."

All week was like that. Hugs, tears, and lots of donations for the memorial. And the best part was, I didn't hear anyone talking about Wilfrido or Pipo Place anymore. I think Wilfrido noticed, because he mentioned Abuela's passing in a newspaper interview. When Aunt Tuti read the article, she reached a new level of hysterics I hadn't known existed.

The week went by fast. In between planning for the memorial, my mom made good on her promise. We all spent time together doing things Abuela enjoyed. The only part I really didn't like was when my dad came home with Abuela's urn. I felt a lump in my throat and couldn't believe Abuela was stuck in that vase forever.

Carmen suggested we scatter her ashes, and I agreed it was a good idea.

"But we might get in trouble," I said.

"So? What are they going to do? Make us scoop the ashes back into the urn?"

I laughed. She had a point.

Wilfrido Pipo tried to reach out to my mom, but that didn't go very well for him. She almost slammed the door in his face a few times, and I think he finally realized that he wasn't invited to the memorial dinner.

"That's not very neighborly of you, Ms. Chef."

"We're not neighbors," my mom said coolly. "You don't live in this neighborhood. Plus, I know you only want to come as a publicity stunt."

Wilfrido cursed and said we'd be sorry after the vote.

It was strange, but Wilfrido's empty threat didn't bother me. The whole week was a love fest for Abuela, and nothing could make those good feelings go away.

Not even when I found out that the Martí photograph Carmen and I had found in Abuela's apartment wasn't real. Mop's dad said it was a very convincing look-alike, but the photo just wasn't old enough and Martí had never stopped at Canal Grove. When I gave my mom the photo and told her the bad news, her reaction surprised me.

"Oh, I remember this. Your aunt and uncle and I were just kids," she said. "Abuelo dressed up as José Martí one year and read poems during dinner at the restaurant. It was so much fun."

She hugged me and ran her fingers through my hair. Then she grabbed my face and kissed my forehead.

22

slicing and dicing

SUNDAY HAD FINALLY come, and my mom and I got to La Cocina really early to start prepping for Abuela's big memorial later that night. The other cooks and chefs, including Martín, were scheduled to come in a little later, so my mom and I were at the restaurant alone.

"Ready?" my mom asked. It was weird that the restaurant was totally empty, because someone was *always* in there. My mom hit the code for the alarm, and I flipped the lights on in the kitchen. The gas stoves flared up. My mom brought out the kitchen knives and placed the assorted ingredients on the prep station.

"We're going to cook *all* of Abuela's best dishes," she

said, sharpening her knife and motioning for me to grab an apron. I gulped.

My mom handed me an onion, a pepper, some plantains, cilantro, carrots, shallots, and something that looked like an onion.

"That's chayote, Arturo. We're going to sauté it, but you need to julienne it first. Do the same thing with the carrots, and make sure to wash the onion with cold water before you cube it. Then go into the walk-in and pull out the veal stock. It needs to get to room temperature to make the broth for the oxtail."

My head spun.

Chef Mom continued. "Don't cut the plátanos, but do peel the boniato and put them in the pot over there. It will be boiling, so don't *throw* them in. The last thing I need is for you to burn yourself. The oxtail is in the walk-in. Bring it to me when you're done."

I stared.

"¿Qué?" she snapped.

"I . . . what is Juliette again?"

"Julienne, Arturo. Julienne. It's sliced long ways and thin. Like this."

She shredded the little orange stick monsters into pieces with her furious chopping. If my mom wasn't a chef, she could have been a samurai. She grabbed a tray full of little chickens and started hacking them in half with a butcher knife that was so big, it looked like it belonged to Conan the Barbarian.

"We're going to make guinea hens," my mom said, cracking them in half in one stroke. She could have easily taken out an army of chickens if they ever attacked her.

I stared at the different colored vegetables in front of me. I had already forgotten what I needed to do.

"Arturo, are you cutting the vegetables?"

"Yes," I said, because a five-foot-five-inch lady with a butcher knife the size of her forearm was very intimidating. My mom moved frantically around the kitchen, prepping and chopping and smelling the cazuelas starting to bubble on the burners. It was impressive.

Abuela and I used to cook together, but her pace was much slower, at least with me. From the time I was six, I stayed with her on Saturday nights while my parents went out, and together we prepped for Sunday family dinner. She would chop vegetables and I would peel potatoes. Together we made soups and sauces and all kinds of cool stuff. Every Saturday night, her apartment filled with the heavenly smells of saffron, yerba buena, cilantro, and perejil. That was our tradition until she got sick and my mom took over the dinner. She preferred to handle everything herself.

I started chopping and peeling and julienning. And then I realized I was crying. And my eyes were burning and they wouldn't stop. I rubbed them and they stung more and my nose started dripping. Before I could reach for a towel, my mom wiped my face with a warm cloth.

"Mom, my eyes are burning!"

I splashed cold water on my face and wiped myself with the towel. I tried to refocus, when I saw my mom crouched over the sink next to me.

"Mom? You okay?" I regained my vision and saw that she was letting water from the faucet slowly run through her fingers. Her head was bowed like she wanted to put it under the faucet as well.

"Mom?"

She looked up, revealing red and puffy eyes.

"Did the onion get you, too?" I asked.

She let out a laugh that sounded more like an exhalation, and her lower lip started to shake. It wasn't an onion. My mom was crying.

I handed her the towel, and she dipped it in the running water and ran it over her face.

"Gracias, mi amor," she said as she hung the towel over her shoulder. "It's been so hard. I'm sorry. You shouldn't have to worry about this. Come on—let's finish, okay?"

My mom put both hands on her face and stretched her cheeks. It was the first time I had ever seen her like that.

She went over to the lobster stock and poured it through a sieve to sift the chunky bits out and pour only liquid into the pot. Then we placed it in another pot and put it back on the burner. I turned the knob, and the flame sparked before calming. The pot steamed slightly.

My mom asked me to grab the fish and clams and mussels out of the walk-in to make seafood paella. I looked up to see the vent twirling. It sent out freezing air, and if I reached my hand up, I could feel my hands turn icy. How awesome would it be if I had the power to turn things into ice? I could have frozen the stupid disease that had slowly messed up Abuela's lungs. I could've frozen my mom's tears. I stepped out of the walk-in, carrying the tub of seafood, and then slapped the tub onto the metal table.

My mom hunched over the lobster stock, and I saw a locket dangle from her neck. The shiny little cross and oval-shaped pendant swayed as if a tiny wind blew them together. My mom smelled the stock, and I listened to the silver cross lightly chime with the pendant. It was Abuela's.

23

cooking from memory

MARTÍN AND A few of the cooks arrived as my mom and I finished cooking. We placed little filets with crispy onions on platters and scooped blue cheese mashed potatoes into serving bowls.

The pescado a la sal had hardened perfectly. It looked like the fish was wrapped tightly in a salt cocoon. My mom said fish cooked that way always came out exactly how fish should taste. We made a little tomato-based sauce to go with the fish, and then we took the guinea hens and oxtail and arranged them in a ceramic serving dish. For appetizers, we made plantain chips, crispy yucca fries, and bacalao fritters.

There were all kinds of salads: salads tossed with

green mango, papaya, strawberries, oranges, everything. We cooked up little masitas de puerco, which were basically little fried balls of pork. We had enough food to feed twenty square blocks.

Next, my cousins arrived and started to take the trays of food to the dining room and patio. Cars parked in the now-infamous lot, and people who loved Abuela made their way inside.

Brian had printed out a huge photo of Abuela and placed it at the entrance of the patio. We kept the front closed so people would have to come in from the lot. My dad wanted everyone to see Abuela before they entered to eat.

"Hey," Carmen said behind me, slouching and smiling. Little drops of sweat covered her nose and it made her freckles look bigger.

"The food smells delicious!" she said.

"Thanks," I said. More cars pulled up, and a few people approached with bags and balloons and flowers. Mr. Michaels carried a stack of books and gave them to us. Chuchi came dressed like she was at a gala. Enique presented my mom with a beautiful portrait of Abuela. Friends and friends of friends showed up by the dozens. The Dominguez family brought about fifteen people (and three bags of heirloom tomatoes) to the memorial dinner. It was awesome.

Carmen had her hair in pigtails and wore bright-green

jeans with a yellow-and-white tank top. I could tell she had been hanging decorations off the trees, because of the little twigs and leaves stuck in her hair.

"Come—I have something to show you," she said. She took my hand and led me outside. "Okay, close your eyes."

Before I did, I looked at Carmen. It was around eight o'clock and the sun was finally setting against the purplish sky. Her eyes were bright with flecks of honey color in them—almost like a radioactive beehive.

Like she requested, I closed my eyes.

"Open them."

She pointed to a floribunda bush. Carmen caressed the small bud and stood back to admire it.

"How did you get it over here? The nursery is at least five blocks away."

"I had a little help from Vanessa and the Green Teens." Carmen opened her arms in triumph. "You like it?"

I looked at Carmen and admired the fully bloomed roses. Then I stared at one rose in particular. It was a white rose. Like the one I'd seen at Abuela's funeral.

"Arturo, you okay?" Carmen asked.

I didn't answer. I just stared as more guests filed into the restaurant. Abuela's favorite music played from the speakers Brian had set up inside.

As everyone ate and danced and laughed, it almost felt

like the old days—like Wilfrido Pipo had never stepped foot in our neighborhood. Only Abuela could create this feeling.

When the memorial was over, everybody helped clean up. My family. Our neighbors. Nobody complained—we were all happy to do it. Abuela would have loved to see this.

After taking out the last bag of garbage, Vanessa came over to say good-bye.

"I never got to tell you, but I am very impressed with your commitment, Arturo. Very impressed."

"Thanks."

"You should run for student council next year. I could use a tenacious spirit on my team."

I stared blankly. "Um, I'll think about it. . . ."

Before she walked out, Vanessa turned around and handed me a flyer.

"I'm going to hold a sit-in tomorrow morning in front of the restaurant. Before the vote."

"Why?"

Vanessa looked at her phone and scrolled through it. "You forget, primo," she said. "I'm a Zamora. Giving up is not in my nature. I sent a message out to five of the youth groups I belong to."

"Wow, that's a lot of people."

"My intel tells me Wilfrido plans to have a bulldozer on the lot first thing in the morning. We're going to be there to make sure he doesn't try anything."

"Okay?" I said.

"These groups *all* live for good old-fashioned advocacy."

I was really proud of my cousin and slightly intimidated she wanted me to join her political activist team at school next year.

Vanessa finally left, and Mop's parents were the next to say good-bye to me. Mop's dad started by handing me a letter.

"I'm sorry he couldn't make it, Arturo. We got buried in work and just couldn't get up there. He was really bummed."

"That's okay," I said, taking the letter.

"He really misses you, Arturo."

"Me too," I said.

"Your food was delicious, by the way. Abuela would have been proud," he said, patting my shoulder.

"Thanks."

Mop's dad put his arm around Mop's mom, and they walked out of the restaurant to their car.

I found Carmen as I got to the lot. It was empty, only a few cars still parked. The streetlamp on the corner was the only light shining on us. I thought about the first time Carmen and I were there. Uncle Frank joined us outside.

"Delicious food, Arturo."

"Thanks," I said.

He gently rubbed my hair. "An incredible chef," he said, looking at Carmen. "Just like Abuela. ¿Verdad, mi amor?"

Carmen nodded, and I dug my hands into my chef's apron as deep as they could go. My throat and stomach took turns dancing and twirling with the rest of my organs. It was a salsa party of nerves, embarrassment, and maybe, kind of, excitement.

"Oh, I forgot to give this back," I said, and handed Carmen her book of poems, which I had tucked into my apron so I would remember to return it.

"Oh, you found my book!" she said, then thanked me.

"Yeah, it was, um, inside one of the mailboxes," I lied.

Carmen took the book and waved good-bye.

After the memorial I went straight home to read Mop's letter. It was exactly how I wanted to end my night.

Hey, Arturo!

What's up? Sorry we haven't talked.

I'm only allowed to use the camp phone once a week because we're supposed to be communing with nature!

Camp is pretty cool. Lots of interesting people. Mostly they're from Georgia and North Carolina and north, north Florida. Like the panhandle. Our camp cabins have no AC, and you can't leave the windows open at night because the mosquitoes will murder you!

Did you hear about Bren? He mailed me a picture of his girlfriend who he met the first day he got to the Dominican Republic, but it was taken from, like, thirty yards away and she wasn't even looking at the camera.

The girls here are really into the outdoors. There's this cool girl, Autumn, who wears a bandanna and she knits. Can you believe that? A thirteen-year-old girl who knits and wears a bandanna? She's so mature. Like, she could be a manager at a coffee shop or something.

Anyway, I'm thinking of wearing sandals more and combing my hair into a bun. Do you think Autumn would be into that? I don't know. It's weird to think about this stuff. Like, three months ago we were happy hanging out on Saturdays and playing ball all day. Now we're thinking about girls all the time. I don't know about you, but it hurts my head. Maybe I'll buy some yarn for Autumn for her knitting. What do you think?

Anyway, hope the restaurant kicks Wilfrido's butt in the bid. See you in a few weeks!

Your bud,
Benjamin "Mop" Darzy

24

ready to roll call

THE DAY OF the vote, I sprang out of bed before my Hulk alarm clock went off. I got dressed and rushed out of my room to leave for the public forum. My mom was already in the kitchen, pacing as she read her notes while my dad coached her. She wore a blue pantsuit, and her hair flowed in swirls down her shoulders. She looked serious and really, really pretty at the same time.

My dad wore khakis and a button-down. I thought that maybe I was underdressed, with my nice jeans and polo shirt, but my mom insisted I looked fine. To be honest, I was glad, because the ninety-five-degree heat in the summer was awful, and all I could deal with was my loose-fitting jeans.

"We'll go ahead and save seats for everyone," my dad said.

There was a knock at the door, and when I saw who it was through the peephole, I almost banged my knee on the door as I opened it.

"Are you okay?" Carmen asked, but I was distracted. She was amazingly well dressed, in a light-pink jacket with a ruffled shirt underneath. I suddenly felt the urge to change again.

"I'll be right back," I said, and stormed into my room. I threw on my khakis, put on a button-down shirt, clipped on a red-and-blue tie, and slid my feet into a pair of loafers. In the bathroom, I soaked my hair and combed it as best I could, then put a lot of extra deodorant on. Not Mira Bro! That stuff is nasty.

I couldn't get my hair to stay down, and after a couple of pats I just gave up and went back outside to meet Carmen. My mom looked at me as I walked out, and gave a suspicious *hmm*.

"Tienes agua en tu camiseta," my mom said.

I looked at my shirt and saw the splotches of water that had soaked through. Carmen giggled.

"I'll go change," I said, but my mom insisted there wasn't time.

"In this heat it'll dry in five minutes," she said, and grabbed her purse and keys and walked out with us. "Carmen ¿tu papá viene con nosotros?"

"No, madrina. Va a ir luego."

The way my mom and Carmen spoke Spanish so easily to each other made me wish I could speak it better.

The restaurant was on the way to the public forum. We didn't plan to stop there, but there was a lot of commotion on the lot, so we took a detour to investigate. As we got closer, we saw about forty of Vanessa's friends sitting in next to a bulldozer. My mom walked up to the construction worker and told him he had no right to park his vehicle there.

"Oh yes, he does!" said Wilfrido, popping up in a golf cart that looked like a Hummer. He wore sunglasses that covered his entire face and the loudest, brightest outfit I had ever seen. It looked like a bag of Skittles had melted and someone had made a suit out of it.

"This is still property of La Cocina de la Isla," my mom said. "So remove your bulldozer."

"Last I checked, this property belongs to the *city*. Not to your family. First thing tomorrow I'll start building. And then the restaurant will be on borrowed time—like an asteroid on a collision course with the earth."

My dad squeezed my mom's shoulder. He whispered something into her ear and then turned to face Wilfrido. My dad was about six-foot-two, and while he was probably the least violent guy ever, he could look pretty imposing. His big hands and huge shoulders and bushy beard made him look like he lived in the mountains with bears.

He bent over Wilfrido's golf cart and said something to him that sent the cart zooming toward the bulldozer. Within a few seconds the bulldozer revved up and backed out of the lot. We all admired my dad like he was Thor or something. He smiled big and took my mom's hand.

"What did you tell him, Dad?" I asked.

"I gave him advice," he said, and winked. "Come on— let's get to city hall."

We marched toward city hall in huge numbers. It felt like we were an army. Actually, we were more like a rising tide during a hurricane—picking up speed and more waves (our family, neighbors, and friends) as we hurled to shore.

When we got there, my mom hurried into the chamber, where she'd make her final plea.

"What are we going to do now?" Carmen asked.

"I don't know," I said. "Let the council vote, I guess."

Carmen found her dad, and I walked to my mom, who greeted people from the neighborhood as they found seats.

The seven city council board members called order, and the room quieted down.

It was all very formal and organized. There was a table that curved out to face residents, and two podiums positioned to face the board members. Each board member had a microphone and a nameplate.

The guy in the middle, who I learned was the chairman of the committee and whose name was really hard to pronounce—Porfirio Mondalla—wore glasses at the edge of his nose and read from a paper. I had never seen him before, and I wondered how he had become chairman of a committee like this.

The other six members flanked him on either side, and I heard each of their names as a lady at the far corner of the table called roll into the microphone. You had to really look, because it seemed like she didn't move her mouth. Her face was expressionless. Like she had done this a million times before.

"Mr. Porfirio Mondalla?" the lady said, and it sounded like she totally butchered his name.

"Here," said Mr. Mondalla.

"Ms. Roberta Mancini?"

"Here," said a lady to the right of Mr. Mondalla. She had to lift herself to the mic from her seat. She seemed younger than the rest of the board members.

"Mr. Gustavo Pérez?"

"Here." Mr. Pérez sported the most epic mustache I had ever seen. I couldn't tell where his nose ended and where his lips began.

"Mr. Eric Anderson?"

"Here."

"Ms. Samaya, um, Crast, Cratanetty?" The lady announcing roll call was trying to pronounce *Crastanetty*.

"Here."

"Mr. Ernesto Bustamante?"

"Ahem, here. Thank you."

"Mr. Tomás García?"

Commissioner García leaned into the mic. I suddenly felt uneasy. I didn't know where we stood with the commissioner.

Next, the chairman read from an agenda for today's proceedings. He read the legal details of the proposal.

"Land Developer Wilfrido Pipo of Pipo Place submitted an additional amendment concerning the property on 426 East Main Street and the adjacent half acre of city-owned property. . . ."

My mind wandered while Chairman Mondalla's voice droned on. It was strange hearing how a place that held real memories and had real people working and eating inside of it for so many years was nothing but an address and a property line to the board members. If there was no personal connection to the place, how could we ever expect to win?

Chairman Mondalla asked whoever was going to speak to stand up to be sworn in. My mom nudged me and whispered, "Stand up with me."

My heart raced. Why did my mom want me to stand? There was no way I was going to speak at the podium! Before I could object, my mom pulled me up, and we both swore before the council that we were going to speak the whole truth and nothing but the truth so help me God.

At that point I didn't even know if God could help me. A few others stood to be sworn in, like Annabelle, as well as Dulce Dominguez, Mr. Michaels, both of Eddy Strap's parents, Chuchi, Enique, Ms. Patterson, and a few others who I didn't see because I was so nervous. And it didn't help that the room was so cold! It was easily ten degrees colder than Abuela's apartment.

Chairman Mondalla explained that the board would hear from the two proposal candidates first and then from the members of the community who'd been sworn in.

Because city council members are elected by the citizens of the county, members would take these opinions into consideration before voting. I learned from Vanessa that the council members must "represent the interests of their constituents." I think that just means that if people felt that council members weren't representing them, they could vote them out in the next election. So maybe it did matter what we said in this room today.

My mom looked over her notes and then up at the clock a few times.

"Mom?"

"¿Sí?" she replied.

"You don't expect me to say anything, right?"

"Shh, they're starting."

Chairman Mondalla looked around the room. "Is Mr. Pipo here?"

Wilfrido had still not arrived, and I wondered if he was going to show up at all. Maybe he was so confident he'd win, he didn't feel like he needed to bother. But then the main doors flew open. It was Wilfrido.

"I have arrived," he said. "Is it my turn yet?"

Wilfrido walked down the aisle, shaking everyone's hands while his assistant, Claudio, handed out postcards featuring Pipo Place. Wilfrido took his seat opposite my mom, and straightened his insanely bright jacket. Slowly, he removed his enormous sunglasses.

"Now that both finalists are here," Mr. Mondalla began, "let us listen to their opening statements for the development of city-owned land for public or private use. We would like to call Wilfrido Pipo to address the room."

Wilfrido took to the podium and cleared his throat about twenty times, then smiled. His sunglasses stuck to his mountain of gelled hair, and his collar was popped so high, it shot up across his cheeks and almost covered his ears. He rolled up his jacket sleeves and began.

It was hard to read the room. Some nodded at what Wilfrido said. Like Eddy Strap's parents and, surprisingly, Ms. Minerva, too. Others like Chuchi and Estelle shuffled uncomfortably in their seats.

"So," Wilfrido concluded, "Pipo Place has many ways to make the community better and bring in money. So when you make a decision, make it for Pipo Place."

People clapped, including Commissioner García and Mr. Bustamante. But I don't know why. It seemed like Wilfrido was trying to play it cool—like he was trying not to come off as desperate. But he came across as lazy instead. I sank into my seat and crossed my arms. Partially because I was freezing in the chamber and partially because I was upset that Commissioner García, of all people, had clapped for such a ridiculous argument.

Wilfrido strutted back to his seat. My mom was next. She took measured steps up to the podium. She shuffled her notes, and the sound of rustling paper echoed throughout the chamber. My heart beat fast. I could hardly hear anything but the *thump, thump* inside my ears while my mom cleared her throat and made her final case for La Cocina.

25

my sugary fate

BEFORE TODAY, IT was safe to say that my mom was not comfortable in the spotlight. It was really hard for her to be in front of people. She was always more comfortable in the kitchen, inventing new twists to Abuela's classic recipes. In that space, she floated swiftly like a bird between the gas stoves and ovens and walk-in refrigerators. Totally confident. The dining room was a different story. My mom always relied on Abuela's charm. But she didn't have that option anymore. She was in charge fully now, and I think that flipped a switch in her. Her voice boomed through the speakers and filled the chamber.

"After an early successful restaurant venture called

La Ventanita," she began, "Veronica and Arturo Zamora (the first) moved here and built a new restaurant on Main Street. For nineteen years this restaurant has grown with the people of Canal Grove. La Cocina de la Isla has hosted weddings, bar mitzvahs, quinceañeras, first communions, and holiday parties. It is both a place where couples go to have a nice night out and a place where you can bring your entire family for a good meal. With the expansion into the lot, we plan to add dining space so we can feed more of you, and we will also increase our space for events. We hope to hold community concerts on a new custom-built stage."

"Pipo Place will offer entertainment, not just concerts," Wilfrido blurted out. "A movie theater, a gym, a spa, a rooftop cocktail lounge!"

Chuchi stood up and hushed him so my mom could continue.

"La Cocina de la Isla belongs to the neighborhood. By building into the lot, we will be a destination for even more people. There is an opportunity to continue to serve the community we love and attract tourists who want to experience Miami beyond South Beach. If this week's closure is any indication, we are still as relevant as ever."

"People want new! People want exclusive!" Wilfrido interrupted again. "People want a VIP experience, not dusty décor and uninspired recipes."

"Quiet!" Enrique yelled out.

"Our business has turned a profit for years," my mom said. "We are financially viable, and we have returned some of those profits to you in a number of ways. This is a matter of *community*. I would like every person in this room to think about what kind of neighborhood they want to live in. Because Wilfrido is right. His vision for Canal Grove is very different, and it would only be the beginning. Thank you."

There was applause, but I noticed not one of the council members clapped like they had for Pipo Place. My mom took her seat, and I squeezed her hand as the members called for a break.

"After the recess, the public will have the opportunity to speak for or against any project."

We all walked outside and gathered around some benches.

"¡Ese imbécil! Interrupting you like that." Aunt Tuti took my mom's hand and rubbed it. "You did great, hermana. I have never been so proud to be a Zamora."

My mom looked completely caught off guard by Aunt Tuti's praise. I didn't think she could remember the last time her sister had given her a compliment.

I saw Carmen by the doors and went over to talk to her. I asked her how she thought it went, and she paused. I figured she thought the same thing I did. The council members clapped louder for Pipo Place. But the community came to my mom's defense when Wilfrido stepped out of line.

"You should speak," Carmen said.

"No way," I said. "I have zero public speaking skills."

"That can't be true. Look at your mom," she said. "You must have some of that in you."

Carmen followed me down a lengthy set of stairs. We walked alongside city hall and past an old fountain that had a statue of one of the city's original founders in it. The fountain was totally dry. I looked in and saw someone inside.

He hummed in between sniffles. Carmen and I stepped into the fountain and walked around the statue to where Wilfrido Pipo's assistant, Claudio, sat, his knees curled into his chest, eating a dessert. He turned around when he saw us.

"You see?" Claudio said as he held up a white container. "I am eating dessert. ¡Tres leches!"

"What's wrong with tres leches?" Carmen asked.

Claudio scraped the last pieces of cake soaked in sugary milk into his mouth. "What is wrong with tres leches? What is wrong with *tres leches*?"

We both nodded.

"I haven't had sugar in two years. Wilfrido is a total control freak. He forbids his assistants from gaining even one pound. Do you know how much sugar is in tres leches? *Do you?*"

"A lot?" I said.

"*A. Lot.*" Claudio shook his head and mumbled.

"What happened?" I asked.

Claudio began to tell us that Wilfrido had just fired him.

"Why?"

"Because I didn't bring enough postcards of Pipo Place and because I didn't defend him when people told him to be quiet in the hearing. But he was interrupting, you know? It was inappropriate!"

"Well, you're right, actually," I said.

"Really?" he said as he looked up, a piece of tres leches dangling from his mouth. "You know, I hope you guys win."

We left Claudio to savor the aftertaste of his hard-earned dessert, and returned to the council chamber.

"This is about a lot more than just our family," I told Carmen. "It's about what's best for the neighborhood."

"You should go up and say that," Carmen said.

"But will the members listen?" I asked. "Will they care?"

Carmen pulled me close. "Convince them," she said. My heart beat fast and my cheeks burned with nervous energy.

"You think I can?"

"Absolutely," she said.

I didn't know what it meant. I didn't know what I was

exactly supposed to feel, especially since she'd never actually told me she liked me, liked me. Maybe she just thought of me as family. I was still pretty much an epic failure in the love department.

"I never told you I'm sorry for, you know, my running off at the festival," she said.

"It's okay," I said.

"It's just . . . nobody had ever said they liked me before."

"I find that very difficult to believe, Carmen."

"It's true! Maybe because I'm taller than most boys, I dunno, but nobody has ever just flat out told me they liked me."

"Well, I never told anyone I liked them, so I guess there's a first for both of us."

She lifted her eyes to meet mine.

Before I could tell her I hoped we could still be friends, Carmen reached over and kissed me. Like an epic pop. I closed my eyes, and my senses heightened. I could hear the quiet rumble of the street, the people walking around city hall. I could sense everything around me like I had a superpower or something.

Carmen stepped away and watched me like she was waiting for a reaction, but all I could give her was a frozen-solid face. I didn't know what to do or say.

"Arturo?"

"Huh?"

I snapped out of my daze.

"You okay?" she asked.

"Huh? Yeah! Totally. Totally good," I said. "Come on—let's get in there. I'm going to kick some butt!"

Carmen laughed, and we both walked back into the chamber. I took the seat next to my mom again. Then something crazy came over me. I didn't know what it was. Maybe it was Carmen saying she believed in me . . . and, well, that stupendous kiss. Maybe it was the thought that Abuela would be watching me. Maybe it was Abuelo's letters, which spoke of courage. I didn't know, but I decided I'd speak in front of the whole neighborhood.

26

the verse and the verdict

"WE'RE GOING TO hear from the community now," said Chairman Mondalla.

I wanted to wait for the right moment to speak, and I figured it might be good to go at the end so I could have the last word.

Several people spoke about how Pipo Place would be good for the community. Eddy Strap's dad talked about how he thought the grocery store would be in a perfect location. Ms. Minerva talked about the gym and how fantastic the new apartments would be.

"It's just nice to come home after being around kids all day and have amenities like that," she said.

She was my seventh-grade language arts teacher! How could she?

Just when I thought no one in the community would come to our defense, I heard Bicycle Bill speak up from the back of the room. I didn't realize he was here.

"'Bout fifteen years ago, I remember asking Doña Veronica to host my thirtieth wedding anniversary at La Cocina, but she said there wasn't enough room to hold that many people. So she let us use the courtyard at her apartment complex. All we paid for was the food and service. She even let us stay in one of the apartments so we wouldn't have to drive home. For free! That was the last anniversary I celebrated with my Shirley. I'll never forget it." He paused, and his voice got very serious as he continued. "The Zamoras are a generous family and a pillar of this community."

That was the longest time I think anybody had ever heard Bicycle Bill talk. Who knew he had such a strong connection to Abuela and La Cocina? I made a mental note to shake his hand after the forum.

"I agree," Dulce Dominguez said. "Doña Veronica came to my daughter Stephanie's house when my grand-daughter was six months old."

"She brought a huge pot of lentils with her," Stephanie said as she held a toddler. "Doña Veronica told me that the potaje she made was going to keep my beautiful baby healthy and strong. Sophia is three, and she hasn't had so much as a cold, knock on wood. ¡Su comida nos alimenta!"

Stephanie ended by saying that Abuela's cooking—La

Cocina's cooking—literally nourished the community. Hearing that made my heart feel full.

"Mr. Pipo said earlier that Pipo Place was 'exclusive' and 'VIP.' Could we talk about what that really means?" It was Aunt Mirta! I hadn't seen her earlier. I guess she was one of the people who swore in to speak when I was too nervous to turn around. She must have taken an early flight from DC and gone from the airport straight to city hall!

Aunt Mirta's face was stern. She was really tall and easily commanded the attention of the room. She flipped through her yellow legal pad and continued. "According to my research, Pipo Land Holdings, LLC is offering premium rates to residents. However, the average income of residents of Canal Grove is well below the rates intended for Pipo Place. I would like Mr. Pipo to explain what he means when he says Pipo Place is *for the community*? What community is he referring to?"

"Noted," Chairman Mondalla said, and wrote something down.

There was a little commotion as people started murmuring. Chairman Mondalla called order.

Carmen motioned for me to get up. Clearly, she also felt I could ride this momentum. But Eddy Strap's mom beat me to it and explained how Pipo Place would bring couture boutiques to Main Street.

I thought about Wilfrido's now former assistant,

Claudio. Wilfrido didn't care about him or the neighborhood. He cared about himself and his money.

"Last call for anyone to speak," said Chairman Mondalla.

This was it. One last shot.

"I . . . I'd like to say something," I said, digging my hands as deep into my pockets as they could go. One of these days I'd really bust through the lining.

Wilfrido watched me intently as I turned to my mom and smiled.

"Go ahead, young man," Chairman Mondalla said. "State your name, where you are from, and what you would like to say about these two projects."

I took a deep breath and closed my eyes. Abuela's face showed up, surrounded by my whole family, then the canals twisting and turning throughout the neighborhood all the way to La Cocina de la Isla.

I opened my eyes and looked at the council members.

"My name is Arturo Zamora," I began, "and I live in Canal Grove in Miami. I would like to speak in favor of La Cocina de la Isla and its beloved owner, my abuela Veronica Zamora."

I pulled out a folded piece of paper I had been carrying around since that night in Abuela's apartment. I opened it up and stared at the words I had written.

"Um, I wrote this when Abuela, um . . . and I, um,

never read it to anyone. It's not very good but, um, you know, I guess she would have liked me to read it. It's called 'Tuyo.'"

"In the silence I

Um.

I hear a melody.
In the ocean,

Um.

In the ocean of solitude,
I

Ahem, sorry, hang on. Let me start over. . . .

In the silence I hear a melody.
In the ocean of solitude
I sail on a ship to shore where you no
    longer are.
In the heat of a thousand summer days,
I try to cool myself in the shades of
    floribundas,

*the coolness of the earth that you planted for
    us all.*

You nurture and teach.

You bring hope when hope is lost.

*Your journey prepared us for our journeys
    beyond.*

"Gracias, Abuela," I said quietly.

I folded the poem and put it back into my pocket, next to the picture of Abuelo dressed as José Martí.

My mission had been to deliver a speech that would win our case. Instead what I delivered was Abuela's eulogy. And in the end, that was all that mattered.

Chairman Mondalla and the rest of the council members huddled together. Commissioner García shook his head and then nodded. Council member Roberta Mancini said something about Canal Grove's history, and Ernesto Bustamante seemed to agree and then disagree. It was nerve-racking to watch them!

After twenty minutes Chairman Mondalla returned to the microphone.

"The council has decided to deliberate further and postpone the verdict until tomorrow."

A collective "Ahh!" echoed through the chamber.

Wilfrido threw on his sunglasses and shuffled past

us without looking. He was fuming, and I could tell by the way he muttered and bit his lip that he was trying not to lose it.

My mom and I and the rest of my family met outside. I walked over to Bicycle Bill and thanked him.

"Your abuela was the greatest," he said as he hopped onto his bike and turned on his speaker. "La vida es un carnaval" by Celia Cruz filled the air, and a few people danced as they walked down the steps.

"Let's go to the restaurant to eat," my mom said to the rest of the family.

Our cousins who we called cousins but weren't really cousins had manned the restaurant while we'd been at the council meeting. I'm sure they wanted to know what went down.

We walked to the restaurant. A huge metallic Pipo Place sign cast a shadow across the empty lot next to La Cocina. I felt like running up to it and knocking it down—letting it tumble to the ground with the rest of the fancy plans Wilfrido had for my neighborhood. But how could I possibly knock down an eight-foot sign made of metal? The bulldozer had been reparked on the lot. It blocked the entrance to the patio, and my mom called the towing company to have it removed.

"It's parked illegally," my mom said with an innocent, slightly mischievous grin.

She and I waited outside for the tow truck to arrive.

When it finally showed up, the driver tried to hitch the bulldozer to the tow, but he didn't have enough space to get the whole bulldozer onto the truck.

"Gonna need to back up a bit," the guy said.

My mom waved her hands, and I joined her in directing the truck driver. I motioned for him to make a slight turn, but he cut the wheel so hard, it swung the cord attached to his truck. The whole thing tipped onto its side, and my mom and I jumped back.

When the truck regained its balance, the front part of the bulldozer that looks like angry teeth slammed to the ground. The loud crash vibrated from the parking lot and echoed through Main Street. People ran out of their stores to see what had happened. When I turned around, I saw Wilfrido Pipo's eight-foot sign had been flattened and cracked in half.

Dulce Dominguez crossed the street and clapped. Mr. Michaels looked shocked and asked if everyone was all right. My mom had the widest, funniest grin on her face.

"The bigger they are," she said, and wrapped her arms around my waist, "the harder they fall."

Officer Rogelio pulled up in his police car.

"Clearly, that sign is a hazard," he said, and promised Wilfrido would be issued a citation.

"Garbage comes on Mondays!" Aunt Tuti shouted from the patio. "The city will collect it."

We all went inside for lunch. Like always, a few tables had been pushed together lengthwise across the center of the dining room.

I picked a seat as Carmen passed by.

"Gotta go wash my hands," she said as she left her bag on the chair next to mine.

My mom slid into the other seat next to me and gave me this *look* like she knew something was up.

"Well, I approve of her family, so that's good," she said with a smirk.

"Um," I said, reminded about Carmen being my mom's goddaughter. "She's not *family*, though."

"Of course she's family."

A sour taste suddenly nipped at my tongue.

"Arturo, family is not just blood. Family is friendship. Family is community."

"She's not related, related, right?" I asked.

My mom laughed. "No, she's not related, related."

The sourness suddenly turned sweet again. Thank goodness, 'cause that would've been really, really weird.

"I'm very proud of you," she said as she poured some freshly made mint juice into her glass.

"Thanks," I said. "Hey, Mom?"

"¿Sí?"

"What if Wilfrido wins tomorrow? What if the whole neighborhood changes?"

"Things have already changed, Arturo," my mom said. "We'll just keep fighting to protect our place in that change. *You* showed me that."

She took my hand.

"You have Abuela's spirit," she said.

Um, what?

"And Abuelo's romanticism, Mr. I Blush Every Time Carmen Is Near. Eh? Eh?"

My mom squeezed my hand a few times and smirked. Okay, if she knew about the kiss, I was going to throw myself into the ocean.

"I have no idea what you're talking about, Mom," is all I said.

"I love you, Arturo."

"I love you too, Mom."

Happiness settled into her dark-brown eyes.

Carmen returned, and the rest of the family dug into the dishes laid out across the table.

"Why don't you read that poem again?" my mom asked as she clinked her glass to get everyone's attention.

"Um, sorry, Mom. No way."

"Yes way," she said. "Everyone, I think it will be nice if Arturo reads that poem again, don't you?"

Was it my mother's job in life to embarrass the heck out of me? That poem was the result of an extreme emotional situation. It was a one-time thing! I had no desire to ever read in public again. Carmen stared at me and smiled. I wasn't José Martí—I didn't have his mojo—but if I could make Carmen smile like that, then I could totally recite my poem again.

Everyone clinked their glasses in approval when I finished. And Carmen whispered, "That was awesome."

I wondered if I'd ever be able to be near her without my neck flaring up like a boiling lobster.

Uncle Frank waved his cell phone excitedly.

"Arturo, I think I just posted a quote from your poem on our website!"

"Let me see." Carmen took Uncle Frank's phone and inspected. "You did it, Papá! You finally posted something on your own."

Uncle Frank smiled triumphantly.

"I am officially social-media savvy." He took the phone and admired his post. "There aren't any responses yet."

"That's because you posted it three seconds ago, Papá."

We all laughed as we watched Uncle Frank hit refresh and wait for responses to arrive.

After lunch the family dispersed while a few of us, like Martín and Mari, stayed behind to prepare for dinner service. I looked around La Cocina de la Isla. The colorful columns and food and memories were my second home. I thought of Abuela and my family. Of the tree-lined streets and canals that made up Canal Grove. My neighborhood. Change *had* come. But I wasn't worried anymore.

epilogue

A FEW WEEKS after the vote, Mop and Bren came home. We met at the park with Carmen and Vanessa. Bren brought a football to throw around to impress Vanessa, but she totally ignored him. She had packed a picnic for all of us and served this delicious mango juice she'd bought at the new juice bar that had opened up in place of Wilfrido's office.

Did you catch that? Wilfrido's gone. After hearing the community, the city council voted and a new ordinance was passed. Buildings could not be taller than a certain height. Pipo Place didn't fit in with the neighborhood. I couldn't find out where he had gone. Then one day Aunt Tuti came to dinner, all hysterical because she had found out that Wilfrido was running for public office!

"He wants to be city commissioner! Can you believe that? Ay, no. No way. I can't. I. Can't."

"Don't get hyst—"

"Don't say it!" everyone yelled in unison before Brian could finish.

The idea of Wilfrido Pipo running for city commissioner was both ridiculous and terrifying. Whatever his plans, I knew he didn't stand a chance against my family.

Our lease was renewed, and my family started working with a contractor for the expansion almost immediately. Uncle Frank helped out with the planning. In the meantime, we planted floribunda bushes everywhere. Abuela would have loved that.

But back to the picnic. Vanessa, Carmen, Mop, Bren, and I ate and played poker for pastelitos. Bren knew how much Vanessa loved pastelitos, so he kept tipping his cards so she could see. Mop protested because he gets really competitive with card games. "Dude! Stop cheating!"

"I'm just helping her out!" Bren said, and smiled awkwardly, which made Vanessa roll her eyes.

Carmen sat really close to me, and a couple of times our hands touched, which made me eat my sandwich really, really fast. This happened, like, four times, so by the last sandwich, I was so stuffed that I felt like throwing up.

There were only a few weeks left before Carmen and her dad had to go back to Spain. It was hard not to think about that, but Carmen told me she didn't want to spend her last days worrying.

"Like your poem says, the journey prepares us for the 'journeys beyond.'"

Uncle Frank's first ever post ended up getting a ton of likes and comments. He decided to put my entire poem on the home page of their website, which was pretty cool. And the fact that Carmen was quoting *my* poem was epically awesome.

Oh, and I was promoted to assistant junior cold food prep cook! Martín was still my boss, but he wasn't as bad to work for anymore. He continued to punch me in the arm whenever I didn't add enough vinaigrette to a salad or when I didn't put enough ceviche on a plate. He said it was so I would stay alert during my shift, but really I think he just liked to punch me in the arm for random reasons.

Oh, and the letters Abuelo left me? Well, I continued filling the blank pages. It was my way of talking to both of my grandparents.

So here's the thing—life *had* changed in a big way. Abuela was gone, and she'd left a big hole behind. But we had also brought the community together. You could feel it. We were all much closer than before Wilfrido had ripped through town. And my mom made it a point to take more days off. She and my dad went out on dates, like, two or three times a week now. I sometimes heard her giggling though the hallway and, I gotta be honest, it was kind of embarrassing.

Vanessa was accepted to Junior Leadership Summit in Washington, DC, and she said her first order of business would be to change the design of the organization's logo because she said it was offensive to indigenous peoples.

After one Sunday family dinner, when everyone had gone home and it was just my mom, Carmen, and me left to lock up, I looked over at Abuela's urn. Carmen stood next to me as we waited for my mom to finish up in the kitchen.

Carmen followed my gaze and said, "I never understood why we display the ashes of the dead this way."

"She's trapped," I replied. "It's sad when you think of how much Abuela liked going to the beach and gardening outside."

I turned around to find my mom behind us. I prayed that she hadn't heard me say that.

"You're right, Arturo. And I have an idea."

My mom took my abuela's and abuelo's urns and asked us to follow her outside. We walked through the streets toward the canals. We stopped by an old structure that was probably once a tower of some kind. A reminder of Canal Grove's Spanish architectural history. My mom handed me Abuela's urn while she held on to Abuelo's.

"Are you sure, Mom?" I asked.

"They should both flow through this town and out to sea where maybe they'll make it back to the island of their birth."

"Wow, that's pretty deep, Mom."

She smiled and winked. "You're not the only poet around here."

We opened the urns and freed Abuela and Abuelo into the canal.

"That's where they need to be," I said.

My mom nodded, and Carmen smiled as I watched Abuela's and Abuelo's ashes move with the current down the twists and turns of the many canals that made up our beautiful neighborhood.

Pablo Cartaya's Recipes Corner

NOTE: Young people, you are amazing cooks, but please make sure there is adult supervision at all times. An abuela, a tío, a tía, a cousin, a cousin who you call cousin but isn't really a cousin, a family friend. It's about family after all, and food tastes better when cooked together. ☺

Tortilla Española

Difficulty: Easy to medium
Total Time: 45 minutes
Serves: 4–6 people

I learned how to make this from a Spanish chef in Madrid who perpetually smelled of grilled onions. It didn't matter if he was wearing his chef coat or regular clothes. But I have to admit; I didn't mind it all that much. There's nothing quite like the scent of onions sizzling in extra-virgin olive oil.

This is a basic Spanish-style tortilla. It isn't fancy, but it is one of the tastiest dishes around. It looks like it takes hours to make, when in fact it doesn't take long at all. There is one part that is tough, but with a little practice you'll be a pro. Let's begin:

Ingredients

3 peeled russet or Idaho potatoes*
1 onion
5 eggs
Extra-virgin olive oil
Sea salt

*You must call them "patatas," like the Spaniards do or the potatoes will be completely offended. Seriously, potatoes get very persnickety about that. Say it with me: *Pa. Ta. Ta.* ¡Bravo! Now when you peel them, make sure you also peel away any bruised parts of the potato.

Cooking Directions

1. After you've peeled the potatoes (remember no bruises!) cut them in quarters so that they look like imperfect cubes. Set them aside in a bowl.

2. Cut the onion in half and peel off the skin. Dice the onions (which means, cut the halves of the onion very small horizontally and then vertically). Put the onions in a bowl as well.

3. Warm the olive oil in a frying pan over medium-high heat. When the oil is hot (about 4–5 minutes), add the bowl of potatoes (What do we call them? ¡Patatas! You're so good at this) to the pan. NOTE: Please be careful when adding the potatoes to the hot frying pan. Ease the potatoes in to prevent oil splatter. (I told you, patatas are temperamental.)

4. Add the onions to the potatoes and stir them. The olive oil needs to soak the potatoes and onions well. Throw in two generous pinches of salt. Stir again to get the salt on all the potatoes and onion bits. Lower the heat and stir occasionally for about 25 minutes to make sure everything cooks evenly.

5. Crack the eggs in a large bowl and whisk until the egg whites and yolks are thoroughly blended. Add another pinch of salt and continue to whisk.

6. The potatoes and onions should be tender by now. If a fork goes into the potatoes easily, they're ready. Using a large cooking spoon, carefully add the contents of the frying pan to the large bowl of whisked eggs (oil and all). Stir until the potatoes and onions are completely coated in the egg mixture.

7. Transfer the potato-onion-egg mixture back into the frying pan. Don't add more olive oil. Let the mixture cook in the pan on low heat for about five minutes. Check underneath the mixture with a spatula to make sure the bottom is cooking well and the mixture is unifying. Keep checking periodically until the eggs are completely set at the edges and halfway set in the center, and the tortilla easily slips around the pan when you give it a nudge with a spatula. This happens after about 5 minutes.

8. Here comes the challenge: After you check that the tortilla mixture is set (about 5 minutes), cover the pan with a large plate.

Make sure you have some wrist support and something to protect you from getting burned (like a kitchen towel or pot holder). Hold the plate in the center with one hand and flip the pan with the other so you're left holding the plate with the newly flipped tortilla (like a waiter carrying a tray).

9. Place the pan back on the stove and slide the tortilla (the way it is sitting on the plate) back onto the pan. Let it cook for 5 more minutes and then you repeat the flip onto a clean plate one final time.* Ready? One. Two. Patata!!!†

10. Let it cool for about 10 minutes and then enjoy.

*If the transfer didn't go smoothly, don't worry. Shape the mixture with a spatula and bake it in the oven at 350° until it solidifies and cooks fully. Then remove it from the oven and let it cool. You'll get it next time.

†You absolutely must yell "¡PATATA!" if you managed to flip it successfully. It's like the "eureka" for tortilla española makers. You can eat the tortilla warm or let it cool for later. Either way, this dish makes for a delicious breakfast, lunch, or dinner appetizer. (Cut it into cubes and put toothpicks in each cube. Guests will love it! Just don't tell them about your secret word.)

Fricasé de Pollo

Difficulty: Medium to hard
Total Time: About 1 hour
Serves: 4–6

This is one of my mom's specialty dishes, Fricasé de pollo. (Don't tell her I'm letting you in on the family secret. Seriously, she'll go supernova on me if she finds out.)

The smell of sofrito and garlic and herbs wafting from the kitchen feels like home to me, and that is what *The Epic Fail of Arturo Zamora* is about: it's about feeling at home. I learned to cook this one day when my kids begged me to make the dish that my mom makes with chicken and tomato sauce. She was out of town and so I called and asked her for the recipe. She gave me the classic version and then, like Cari in my book, I put a slight spin on it by adding cauliflower rice and using organic ingredients for the chicken and the tomato base. It has a more modern feel but maintains the integrity of the original dish. Here it goes:

First things first: create a playlist to get you in the mood. I suggest Celia Cruz, Benny Moré, or Tito Puente. There needs to be at least one or two rhumba hip shakes before you begin. The fricasé will be ruined if you don't.

Ingredients

3 to 4 pound chicken, cut into serving pieces*

*I prefer organic chicken but it doesn't have to be. Mami uses regular chicken. She calls me, "Mr. Organic who never ate organic food as a kid and now all of a sudden eats organic." I usually buy skinless or take the skin off, but my mom leaves it on. Skin on is more traditional. Skin off gets the juices and marinade right on the meat. Your call. They're both delicious.

For the marinade

1 teaspoon salt

1/2 teaspoon fresh ground pepper

1 teaspoon ground cumin

1 teaspoon dried oregano

1 teaspoon smoked paprika

1 bay leaf

6 garlic cloves, mashed to a paste in a mortar and pestle or
minced

1/4 cup fresh lime juice

1/4 cup fresh lemon juice

1/2 cup fresh orange juice

1 tablespoon olive oil

For the cooking sauce (sofrito)

3 tablespoons olive oil

1 medium yellow onion, finely diced

1 green bell pepper, cored, seeded, deveined, and finely diced

6 garlic cloves, minced

1/4 teaspoon smoked paprika

1/2 teaspoon ground cumin

1/2 teaspoon dried oregano

1 large can of crushed fire-roasted tomato sauce*

1 tablespoon tomato paste

3/4 cup dry white wine

1/3 cup of Goya brand alcaparrado†

2 bay leaves‡

7 or 8 small russet potatoes, peeled and quartered

*Again I prefer organic. Cue Mami eye roll.

†This is a jar of manzanilla olives, pimentos, and capers that
can be found in most Goya food product sections in your local
grocery store. It's the key ingredient to this whole dish, so don't
bypass it.

†This is super important because the bay leaves tie all the other slightly salty and tangy flavors together really nicely.

Cooking Directions

1. Start by marinating the chicken. Place the chicken in a large mixing bowl. Rub the chicken with salt, pepper, cumin, oregano, and paprika. In a small bowl, combine the garlic and bay leaf with the citrus juices and olive oil. Pour over the chicken and mix well. Cover with plastic wrap and refrigerate for at least an hour.

2. To cook the chicken, in a large caldero or dutch oven heat the olive oil over medium heat until it starts to ripple. Scrape the marinade off the chicken, remove the bay leaf and discard, and set the marinade aside. Working in batches so as not to overcrowd the pot, brown the chicken on all sides for about 10 minutes. Remove the chicken and set aside.

3. In the same pot, with any oil that's still left, sauté the onion and green pepper for about 4 minutes, until the onions are translucent. Add the garlic, paprika, cumin, and oregano and cook for another 2 to 3 minutes. Add the tomato sauce and paste and mix well to combine. Add the reserved marinade and white wine and cook, stirring, for another 5 minutes. Add the alcaparrado. Return the chicken to the pot. Add the potatoes. Bring to a boil, lower the heat, and allow to simmer for about 25 to 30 minutes, until chicken and potatoes are fully cooked and fork tender. If the sauce is too watery by the time the chicken is cooked, uncover, raise the heat, and boil until the sauce thickens. Serve with white rice. Makes 4 to 6 servings.

Okay, a note on the white rice. If you avoid rice and other starches, you can substitute cauliflower rice (cue Mami slapping her head and walking away in disgust). But if you do use white rice, one tip I recommend is using a good butter like Kerrygold butter and throwing about ¼ tsp of it into the rice while it cooks. Also add some salt and a dash of olive oil. It brings the rice to a whole other level. ☺

¡Disfruta! Let me know how the dish turns out!

author's note

José Julián Martí y Pérez (January 28, 1853–May 19, 1895), better known as José Martí, was a leader of the Cuban independence movement from Spain and a renowned poet and writer who wrote in both English and Spanish. Martí devoted his life to Cuban independence and firmly believed in the principles of freedom, tolerance, and love. He created a very popular magazine for children (one of the first of its kind in the United States) called *La edad de oro* (*The Golden Age*). *La edad de oro* contained many colorful stories for children as well as poems conveying the message that children are the best hope for the future.

He is best known for his collection of poems for adults called *Versos sencillos*. Several of the verses from this collection were later put to music in a song called

"Guantanamera," which has become one of Cuba's most famous songs. A Spanish composer named Julián Orbón is responsible for the adaptation. He was a teenager living in Cuba in the 1940s when he came up with the idea to combine Martí's words with a popular Cuban melody. The famous folk singer Pete Seeger made Orbón's version a global sensation.

In *Versos sencillos*, Martí describes his admiration of nature, his love of Cuba, the importance of friendship, and his feelings about injustice. These poems reflect very personal experiences, and the book contains many of his best-known poems. It is the reason I wanted Arturo to use verse and the lost art of letter writing to help sort through his emotions. Abuelo's letter to Arturo is partly translated from one of Martí's letters. The original in Spanish is below.

¡Amor es que dos espíritus se conozcan, se acaricien, se confundan, se ayuden a levantarse de la tierra. . . . Nace en dos con el regocijo de mirarse, alienta con la necesidad de verse! ¡Concluye con la imposibilidad de desunirse! No es torrente; es arroyo; no es hoguera, es llama; no es ímpetu, es paz.

ACKNOWLEDGMENTS

Family made this book happen. My wonderful extended family at Viking, led by the amazing Ken Wright, and the entire group at Penguin Random House (yes, all of you), especially the incomparable Joanna Cárdenas, my editor and all-around super ninja. My family at Foundry Literary + Media and my agent, but most importantly friend, Jess Regel, you are nothing short of incredible.

To mentors, friends, colleagues, and places that, in one way or another, helped to shape this story by giving me a sense of home among them: Kathi Appelt, Matt de la Peña, Shelley Tanaka, Joe McGee, Jessica Rinker, Lisa Papademetriou, the Allies in Wonderland, Lou McMillian, Chef Cindy Hutson, Ortanique on the Mile, the city of Coral Gables, the city of Miami, Deborah Briggs, The Betsy-South Beach, the spirit of Hyam Plutzik, and so many more names and places that have touched my life and influenced this. Thank you.

To my immediate family—it's a big one so brace yourselves: To my mother, who told me at nineteen that I would write for children and young adults. You were right, Mami. About that and so much more. I love you. To my father; my brothers, Danny and Guillo; my sisters-in-law, Damary and Kiany; Tía Tati and Yoli;

my cousins and cousins who I call cousins but aren't really my cousins. To my in-laws, Cindy, John, Tom, his partner Joan, my little sisters, Pam and Molly—they are the #bestinlawsever. And to my grandparents, whose presence surrounds us all. Between the joys, tears, sometimes anger and frustration, difference of opinions, arguments, hugs, cheers, and epic parties together, I couldn't ask for a better family. We're not crazy . . . we're colorful. ☺

To my children, Penelope and Leonardo. They're not just great kids, they're wonderful humans. And finally, to my favorite forever: Rebecca, the journey starts and ends with you.